RYOHGO NARITA

ILLUSTRATION BY
SUZUHITO YASUDA

DURARARA!!

DRRR!! 12

WRITTEN
BY
*RYOHGO
NARITA*

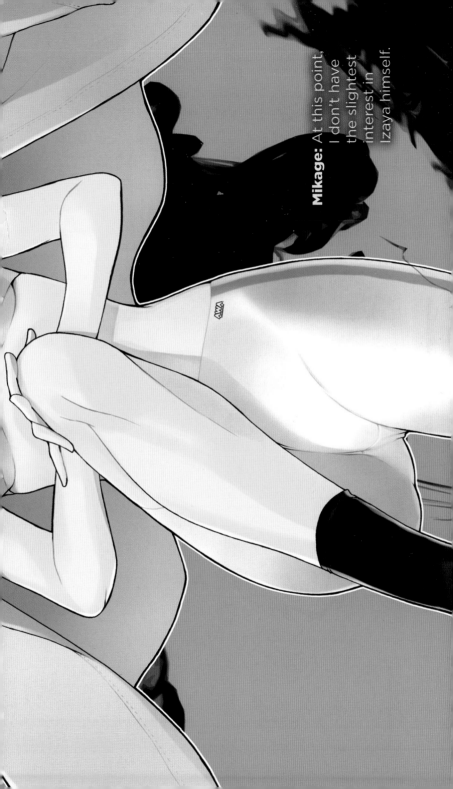

Mikage: At this point, I don't have the slightest interest in Izaya himself.

Mikage: But the fact is, I find the starkness that surrounds him to be oddly comfortable.

VOLUME 12

Ryohgo Narita
ILLUSTRATION BY Suzuhito Yasuda

NEW YORK

DURARARA!!, Volume 12
RYOHGO NARITA
ILLUSTRATION BY SUZUHITO YASUDA

Translation by Stephen Paul
Cover art by Suzuhito Yasuda

This book is a work of fiction. Names, characters, places, and incidents are the product of the author's imagination or are used fictitiously. Any resemblance to actual events, locales, or persons, living or dead, is coincidental.

DURARARA!! Vol.12
© RYOHGO NARITA 2013
First published in Japan in 2013 by KADOKAWA CORPORATION, Tokyo.
English translation rights arranged with KADOKAWA CORPORATION, Tokyo,
through Tuttle-Mori Agency, Inc., Tokyo.

English translation © 2019 by Yen Press, LLC

Yen On
1290 Avenue of the Americas
New York, NY 10104

Visit us at yenpress.com
facebook.com/yenpress
twitter.com/yenpress
yenpress.tumblr.com
instagram.com/yenpress

First Yen On Edition: March 2019

Yen On is an imprint of Yen Press, LLC.
The Yen On name and logo are trademarks of Yen Press, LLC.

The publisher is not responsible for websites (or their content) that are not owned by the publisher.

Library of Congress Cataloging-in-Publication Data
Names: Narita, Ryōgo, 1980– author. | Yasuda, Suzuhito, illustrator. | Paul, Stephen (Translator), translator.
Title: Durarara!! / Ryohgo Narita, Suzuhito Yasuda, translation by Stephen Paul.
Description: New York, NY : Yen ON, 2015–
Identifiers: LCCN 2015041320 | ISBN 9780316304740 (v. 1 : pbk.) |
    ISBN 9780316304764 (v. 2 : pbk.) | ISBN 9780316304771 (v. 3 : pbk.) |
    ISBN 9780316304788 (v. 4 : pbk.) | ISBN 9780316304795 (v. 5 : pbk.) |
    ISBN 9780316304818 (v. 6 : pbk.) | ISBN 9780316439688 (v. 7 : pbk.) |
    ISBN 9780316474290 (v. 8 : pbk.) | ISBN 9780316474313 (v. 9 : pbk.) |
    ISBN 9780316474344 (v. 10 : pbk.) | ISBN 9780316474368 (v. 11 : pbk.) |
    ISBN 9780316474382 (v. 12 : pbk.)
Subjects: | CYAC: Tokyo (Japan)—Fiction. | BISAC: FICTION / Science
    Fiction / Adventure.
Classification: LCC PZ7.1.N37 Du 2015 | DDC [Fic]—dc23
LC record available at http://lccn.loc.gov/2015041320

ISBNs: 978-0-316-47438-2 (paperback)
       978-0-316-47439-9 (ebook)

1 3 5 7 9 10 8 6 4 2

LSC-C

Printed in the United States of America

INTERLUDE

Durarara!! 12 Ryohgo Narita

An excerpt from Shinichi Tsukumoya's closed blog

Let me tell you about Mikado Ryuugamine.
And also about the Headless Rider.

I don't know what it is you seek to know, visitor to this website.
After all, there's been a lot going on lately around the Dollars. Too much, in fact.
As a member of the group, I've done as much information collecting around the periphery as I can.
And what did I find?
A variety of incidents and people intertwined in a complex and tangled game of cat's cradle.
And to continue that metaphor, there are two fingers in particular that are especially tangled up.
Mikado Ryuugamine and the Headless Rider.
Plus, Izaya Orihara and Kasane Kujiragi seem to enjoy tampering with these strings maliciously, so who's to say whether the tangles can be unwound at all?

There are a number of other fingers, to continue this metaphor. Allow me to list off the big ones.

There's Celty Sturluson, as I've already mentioned. She's involved in the highest number of incidents, to be sure, but she's also the central figure of many.

That's right: Her severed dullahan's head has finally taken center stage in public. In the way she wanted least.

The police quickly seized the severed head that had been left on the Ikebukuro sidewalk in broad daylight. The head itself wasn't shown on the news, but it had been exposed all the same.

Celty already had her hands full with her own affairs, but the things around her just wouldn't leave her alone, either:

- The hit-and-run on Kyouhei Kadota, Dollars officer
- The team-up of Mikado Ryuugamine and Aoba Kuronuma, using the Blue Squares within the Dollars to lead a battle against the Yellow Scarves
- The contact between Mikado and Akabayashi, a lieutenant of the Awakusu-kai
- The issue with Haruna Niekawa, wielder of Saika and member of the Dollars
- The attention of Seitarou Yagiri, the president of Yagiri Pharmaceuticals

All these incidents and issues heavily involve the Headless Rider, whether by intention or coincidence.

She does have a few allies, however. In fact, they simply gather at her residence, so it's kind of unclear whether they're honest allies or something else. Mika Harima, Seiji Yagiri, Walker Yumasaki, Saburo Togusa, Egor the suspicious Russian, and his client Shingen Kishitani... I'm not sure whether his wife, Emilia, should be counted, but lastly, there's also Namie Yagiri, who made her way in—and she is certainly *not* a friend. So the Headless Rider has got trouble within and trouble without.

Where is the future taking her, do you suppose?

But the one whose future is even more uncertain is Mikado Ryuugamine.

The founder of our Dollars, the one calling the shots for the Blue Squares—and a mere high school student.

That's right. I'm willing to state that on the record here. Mikado Ryuugamine is a "mere high school student."

He is not an inhuman creature like Celty, and he doesn't have Shizuo Heiwajima's strength or Anri Sonohara's cursed weapon.

He's just a plain old human, pure and simple.

But that's the kind of person—perhaps *because* he is that kind of person—who is now in just as much trouble as Celty, if not even more, because of the following:

- The hit-and-run on Kyouhei Kadota, Dollars officer
- Aoba Kuronuma and his gang, who are trying to use Kadota and the Dollars
- Izaya Orihara and Kasane Kujiragi, and the young man named Hiroto Shijima, who joined the Dollars while having connections to both Izaya and Kujiragi
- Threats from Akabayashi of the Awakusu-kai
- Shuuji Niekawa's request to search for his daughter, Haruna Niekawa
- Mikado's turf war with the Yellow Scarves

...There are more that could be listed, but these are the chief concerns.

Yes, I know what you want to say. It looks almost the same as Celty's list, doesn't it?

But it's not. Their implications are entirely different.

Celty Sturluson was merely *dragged into* all this business, even the part about her own head. Some of that is thanks to her quasi-legal job as a courier, so one might call it expectable, but the way she's been manipulated into all of it is beyond that kind of simple karma.

Meanwhile, for Mikado Ryuugamine, the majority of these issues are seeds *he himself* sowed. He could have refused to deal with the Haruna Niekawa and Shijima issues. He could have murmured passive affirmations and tossed them out afterward.

But Mikado Ryuugamine did not.

He was trying to burn everything down to reset the Dollars, while doing his best to save every single good person who clung to the group.

Good person. Yes, "good person." At least, going by his own standards.

Some of you might wonder why I don't alert him, since I know everything going on behind the scenes.

Yeah, I could. Perhaps I would have given warnings to the "Tarou Tanaka" of a year ago, the guy who was addicted to the Internet to the point that he believed in its power. *Watch out for Shijima; stay away from Haruna Niekawa*—and so on.

But such warnings are pointless to the current Mikado.

He no longer trusts anything online. Not the Dollars, not Anri Sonohara, not Masaomi Kida.

But of course he doesn't. He doesn't even believe in himself—the focal point of all those connections.

And that's why he's trying to burn it all down. To crush it all to dust and cast it aside.

He's trying to erase everything that he's built up to this point. Including Mikado Ryuugamine himself.

There's only one thing he believes in: the past.

The illusion he witnessed when the Dollars first met and all networks seemed to sparkle and shine to him.

That memory has been positively adjusted in his mind. Perhaps it now represents the peak of Mikado Ryuugamine's life to him and acts as the genesis for everything.

Unbelievable. Rather than choosing the bonds of family with his parents, or memories of his best friends, he's decided to make the focal point of his entire life the event in which a group of strangers met in person for the first time.

It's laughable but not funny.

At the very least, I don't have the right to laugh at it.

In this case, I can focus only on being an observer. As you probably know, having found my blog, I learn things a bit quicker than others do, and I have knowledge of various topics.

But I do not know the future.

I like people, if not as much as Izaya Orihara does.

And unlike him, I also like those who *aren't* human.

Which is why I observe.

I'll be honest with you: I can manipulate things by releasing information in the right ways. However, I cannot tell exactly what the end results will be. ·

So helping someone might also mean hurting someone else. It might mean that *something* will happen that will change Ikebukuro forever.

You get it, right?

You know that we stand atop a thin layer of ice held in place only by a fragile balance.

And so do Celty Sturluson and Mikado Ryuugamine and many other people involved with them.

The strings in their game are tied not around their fingers, but around their necks.

And the game of cat's cradle will come to an end soon enough.

Shizuo Heiwajima.

He has already grasped the string.

When he yanks on that string, will everyone it is connected to come out unscathed?

It's not a question of who will laugh and who will cry. It's a question of whether anyone will be *able* to do things like that at the end of this.

Such is the current situation.

It's all a logjam. It's checkmate.

I'm not going to say, "This is getting interesting now." I'm not Izaya Orihara.

It would be more accurate to say, "This is getting troublesome."

I mean, my town is getting turned into one big slow-moving accident. But only a limited selection of people can actually see it happening.

There are the "light of day" folks, the ones hard at work in business or school, shopping at the department stores of Parco, Seibu, and Tobu.

There are the "dark of night" folks, getting up to no good in the back alleys, parking garages of clubs, and seedy apartment rooms.

But the strings of this disaster are tangled around those who belong to *neither* group.

Let's say that Ikebukuro is a map. The folks I'm talking about are not on the front side or the underside of the map, but lodged deep inside the paper fibers in the middle.

I'm not telling you to be careful. I'm telling you to be ready.

Because if that map rips from the inside, it will cause great damage to both sides of the parchment.

But what shape do you suppose it is that this game of cat's cradle has produced?

It is irregular, complex, and in the end, interconnected.

I'm not going to sit here and tell you, "It is the shape of Ikebukuro itself." But I do think it's clear that this is the shape of *something* that makes up this city.

Will the strings burn away, will Shizuo Heiwajima pull off the fingers—er, heads—of those in the middle, or will someone come along and neatly undo all the knots?

All I can do is watch.

But watch I will.

When this "mere high school student" paints himself into a corner, I will see who is dragged into it, how he falls, and where.

I suspect that the story of Mikado Ryuugamine, mere high school student, is coming to an end soon.

But do you know what?

An ordinary student, not even a bully or a thug, calling the shots of a street gang and getting the strings of fate tangled around yakuza and headless motorcycle riders alike?

It sounds just like some urban legend to me.

Celty Sturluson was not human.

She was a type of fairy found from Scotland to Ireland, commonly known as a dullahan: a being that visited the homes of those close to death to inform them of their impending mortality.

The dullahan carried its own severed head under its arm, rode in a two-wheeled carriage called a Coiste Bodhar pulled by a headless horse, and approached the homes of the soon to die. Anyone foolish enough to open the door was drenched with a basinful of blood. Thus the dullahan, like the banshee, made its name as a herald of ill fortune throughout European folklore.

One theory claimed that the dullahan bore a strong resemblance to the Norse Valkyrie, but Celty had no way of knowing whether this was true.

It wasn't that she *didn't* know. More accurately, she just couldn't remember.

When someone back in her homeland stole her head, she lost her memories of what she was. It was that search for the faint trail of her head that had brought her here to Ikebukuro.

Now with a motorcycle instead of a headless horse and a riding suit instead of armor, she had wandered the streets of this neighborhood for decades.

But ultimately, she had not succeeded at retrieving her head, and her memories were still lost.

Celty knew who had stolen her head.

She knew who was preventing her from finding it.

But ultimately, she didn't know where it was.

And she was fine with that.

As long as she could live with those human beings she loved and who accepted her, she could happily live the way she was now.

She was a headless woman who let her actions speak for her missing face and held this strong, secret desire within her heart.

That was Celty Sturluson in a nutshell.

Yes, she was a dullahan.

Celty Sturluson was not human.

She could not become a human, and a human could not become a dullahan.

But still, she did her best to understand what it meant to be human.

She learned about humanity through a variety of things and took great pains to live as a human being did.

A rare and powerful sense of reason built her persona, and despite the lack of a head or legal identity, she gained an almost perfectly human mind and lived as an individual within the city of Ikebukuro in Japan.

Which was why nobody could predict what exactly would happen to a dullahan that had lost not only its memories, but also its sense of reason, whether out of anger, sadness, shock, or pain.

CHAPTER SEVEN
AT DAGGERS DRAWN

Durarara!! 12 Ryohgo Narita

Shinra's apartment

Celty Sturluson's mental state was quite similar to that moment when the circuit breaker trips and the home suddenly goes dark and quiet.

An enemy calling herself Kasane Kujiragi suddenly appeared in their home and locked lips with Shinra Kishitani, the owner of the apartment. At this point, she still had a basic human level of reason remaining.

It was so sudden that it did take some time for her to fully process what had just happened—so that when she finally understood, the next situation was already occurring.

Unnatural blades, extending from Kujiragi's fingers like nails.

Celty instantly recalled when she had seen such a phenomenon before.

Saika!

A cursed blade that controlled those it sliced and that implanted "children" within their minds.

Anri Sonohara was supposed to be in possession of Saika, so how did this woman have it now? Or was this some other, different cursed blade?

These questions and more floated through her mind as the steel sank into Shinra's shoulder.

It felt like time stood still.

Already, Celty was unable to recognize or process the surroundings around them.

"..."

...

...*Huh?*

What?   *What am I seeing?*

A dream?   *Some kind of joke?*

Shinra is here.   *Who is this woman?*

A kiss?   *With Shinra?*   *Why?*

What is this?   *Saika's owner?*   *Cheating?*   *No.*

Thief.   *Must hurry.*   *Kiss?*   *Katana?*

Oh no.   *I've seen this.*   *Saika.*   *Transform.*

Shinra.   *Controlled.*   *Oh no.*   *He must be fine.*

I trust.   *So what?*   *Shinra.*   *Don't.*

Wait.   *Shinra.*   *Shinra is.*   *Shinra must.   No!*

Shinra.   *Shinra.*   *It can't be.*

I hate this.   Shinra.   Please wait.

Shinra.   *Shinra.*   *Shinra, Shinra.*

Why is Shinra   I have   with Shinra   and Shinra   but who   would do

No.   No, no, no.   But I   love Shinra

Shinra   no Shinra   mistake   won't believe it   Shinra   wait Shinra   can't

be   won't let it   don't

StopthatrightatoncetakethatbladeoutofShinraletgoofhimwhywon't
mybodymoveShinraShinraShinraShinraShinraShinraShinraruna
wayrunawayrunawayrunawayrunawayrunawaymoveCeltymove-
movemovemovemoveohnoohnoohnoohnoohnoohpleaseohpleaseo
hpleaseShinraShinraShinraShinraShinraShinraShinraShinraShin-
raShinraShinraShinraShinraShinraShinraShinraShinraShinraSh-
inraShinraShinraShinraShinraShinraShinraShinraShinraohplease
ShinraIShinraloveShinraShinraandShinrayetShinraIShinraloveShinr
aShinraandShinrayetShinraIShinracan'tShinramoveShinraShinraShi
nra————————

The emotions that her confusion dredged up only made the confusion worse.

She was struck by two simultaneous levels of shock—an unfamiliar woman kissing Celty's lover, followed by his being pierced by that woman's blades.

It was the biggest shock she'd felt since losing her head, and it ate away at her rational mind, loosening her grip on reality.

Then she was hit by a third shock:

Before she had time to react, Celty witnessed Shinra's eyes instantly *turn red with blood.*

When Saika stabs you, your eyes turn red.

Subjugation. The fate of Saika's child.

This fact, sinking into her mind, caused something within Celty to burst.

Emotion: a storm of conflicting feelings surging into her panicked brain, suddenly bulging to their maximum possible size.

Celty's instincts began emergency measures to prevent the worst-case scenario: total breakdown.

To save her memory and self-image from the muddy churn of her emotions, she cut rationality loose from her body.

The circuit breaker within her tripped without a sound.

And then…

♂♀

"Wh-whoa, whoa, whoa! What are you doing?!"

It was Togusa who first spoke up in response to the woman's sudden aggressive behavior. He was in the adjacent room, but because he was next to the sliding door, he could see right away what was happening there.

He rushed to pull Kujiragi off Shinra but came to a stop just as suddenly.

"Wha...?"

He had *seen shadows erupting* into the space before him.

"..."

Kujiragi witnessed the phenomenon as well.

There was no longer the shape of a woman in the space where Celty had been standing. It was just a writhing, expanding mass of shadow, brimming with pressure. One might actually be forgiven for imagining a gusher of oil right in the middle of the room.

But the black shadow, somewhere between a gas and a liquid, expanded explosively throughout the apartment and set upon Kujiragi.

"As I expected," the woman muttered to herself as the black mist descended upon her with clear and present hostility. She lifted the listless, red-eyed Shinra over her shoulder and leaped backward with an agility that was simply inhuman.

Kujiragi landed next to Togusa and twisted around. After she had leaped away again, the black mass's jaws closed upon the spot where she'd just been. *Jaws* was the only word to describe them.

They weren't like those of any living creature on the planet, but they did have countless black fangs within them, and they bit with such incredible force that they seemed to sink into the very atmosphere itself. The sight was forceful enough to plunge any who saw it into a state of terror.

Neither Togusa, who along with Kujiragi was the first to witness it, nor those who heard the uproar and came to see what was happening moments later could actually understand what it was they were seeing.

That there was a black shadow with its own physical form should have been enough for them to identify Celty Sturluson, but in the moment, that answer was absent from their minds.

Because in the case of this black mass, there was not a bit of the rationality and intelligence they associated with Celty's typical shadowy manipulations.

Kujiragi raced forward, reaching out, not sparing a backward glance. The next moment, an extremely slender blade like a piece of wire extended from her finger and, with the tensile strength of a whip, lashed in a circle pattern at the glass door to the veranda.

There was the momentary sound of metal scraping, and then a perfect circle fell out from the center of the glass door, just big enough for a person to get through the hole. Without losing any speed, Kujiragi passed through it still carrying Shinra, leaped to the railing of the veranda, and then promptly took flight.

The next moment, everyone left behind in the apartment learned that the giant shadow jaws that had appeared in the bedroom were only a small part of the whole.

A number of other sets of jaws appeared from the room, spinning and churning around the apartment at breathtaking speed. When they identified Kujiragi leaping from the veranda and Shinra slung over her shoulder, they all turned in that direction, then withdrew back to the bedroom.

"Wh-what was that all about...?" Togusa murmured. He tried to peek into the room.

The door of the bedroom—and the entire wall it was set within—erupted, and an enormous mass of shadow leaped out.

"Guwoah—?!"

Togusa didn't get enveloped in the destruction, but the shadow did push him out of the way. The thing then broke down the glass door to the veranda, chasing after Kujiragi, who had leaped off the building with superhuman leg strength.

Shards of glass glittered in the air, surrounding a mass of shadow that had turned into jaws the size of an elephant.

The jaws blended into the darkness of night and made to devour Kujiragi whole, along with Shinra, too. But just an instant before they could, Kujiragi's body somehow accelerated in midair.

The wire-width Saika extending from her hand tangled with the metal fence on the roof of the building across the street, and she used it like a winch to pull herself faster across the way.

The shadow missed its prey. But rather than falling down to the street below, the pursuit maintained its intensity. Ten shadow tentacles extended from the main body and lashed out at Kujiragi with the force of crossbow bolts. But the woman did not so much as grimace.

Instead, she landed on the rooftop and withdrew the wire-form Saika into her palm. The part of the fence Kujiragi had tangled it around sliced open and fell to the ground, a dry clatter against the night sky.

As if on cue, Kujiragi held out her right hand toward the shadow tentacles chasing her. It could only be the right hand, because Shinra was still slung over her left shoulder.

Five blades appeared from her fingertips again, forming a large vortex in the direction of the black limbs. A whirlwind of five narrow blades.

No ordinary blade would be capable of blocking this strange shadow with physical properties. But Saika was no ordinary blade. This accursed weapon could probably slice through the human soul itself, if you believed in such things. And in fact, it excelled at damaging the mind, which was very close to the soul, so that it could infiltrate it.

A physics-transcending shine of silver met a physics-transcending shadow of solid matter.

After a hideous sound of intense friction, the whirlwind of blades cut through all the attacking tentacles, turning them back to mist.

But the body of the shadow did not give up. Even as it fell, it created new shadow feelers that grasped for Kujiragi. She swung back against all of them, racing across the rooftop with superhuman speed.

♂♀

"Owww... What was that about?"

The shattered glass was sprayed about the veranda, allowing the muggy air of the summer night into the apartment.

Togusa got to his feet, rubbing his lower back. What was that black *thing* just now?

Ordinarily, the sight of a writhing black *thing* in this apartment would lead everyone to the same answer. In this place, in this entire neighborhood, only one person could make use of a 3-D moving shadow.

But Togusa's brain was unable to make the connection at the moment. What he had just seen had *held no trace of human form.*

The sight of the shadow mass taking a form that wasn't that of a human or of any living creature had caused Togusa to think some kind of unknown monster had suddenly appeared in the room with them.

He felt not a single trace of the emotion and personality he'd always associated with that moving shadow.

"Hey, Yumasaki, what the hell just…?"

"Ohhh… Ohhhhhhh…"

Togusa turned to look at Yumasaki, who was gazing out the window and moaning queerly.

"What's up, Yumasaki? Did you hit your head?" he asked.

Just then, Yumasaki raised his arms high and shouted in jubilation, "My time…my era has arrived at laaaast!"

"What the hell do you mean?!"

"A mysterious babe wearing glasses…strange wires coming from her hand…cutting a circle in the glass… A heroine who leaps through the sky, fighting the aliens dyed black! It's all perfect! She was a bit older than I imagined, but at last, it's the arrival of the 2-D heroine who will open a new door in my life!"

Yumasaki was so wrapped up in his own world that it was hard to tell whether he was even aware of Togusa. He continued shouting up to the open sky. "I must cause my own power to awaken soon! I bet kissing my little sister will cause that woman to be 2-D again, even if she's temporarily in a 3-D form right now!"

"Okay, forget this guy." Once Yumasaki got this way, Togusa knew there was no way to hold a conversation with him. It would be difficult to pull him back to reality without Kadota, but at least Yumasaki didn't have the synergistic effect of Karisawa's presence.

"Dammit, and I gotta go visit Kadota first thing in the morning tomorrow."

Yumasaki's typical mood was possible only because Karisawa

had just texted him the news that Kadota was awake again. Even *he* wouldn't let himself get this carried away without the relief of such good news. Or at least, that was what Togusa wanted to believe.

Once his mind had calmed down, Togusa realized that the thing that had flowed out of the room had probably been Celty's shadow, and he hesitantly peered into the bedroom.

"Um, hey, Celty, was that your...?" he started to say, then stopped.

The room was devoid of life. The only notable thing within it was the helmet Celty always wore, resting on the ground.

"...Hey, what does this mean?"

"Celty just left," answered Mika Harima, who was looking outside through the shattered glass doorframe.

"What? But what does *that* mean?"

"That black thing that just burst out of the apartment... That was Celty."

"..."

Togusa fell silent. It wasn't that he couldn't have imagined this. He just didn't want to actually consider it.

The Headless Rider whom Togusa knew, contrary to her fearsome appearance, was just as smart and reasonable as Kadota, tops among people he knew.

But there hadn't been anything resembling the Headless Rider he knew in that dark monstrosity just now, and there was no glimmer of reason or wisdom in the wake of its destruction.

"Oh my, this is the after of exactly what event being revealed?"

This absurd attempt at the Japanese language was accompanied by Emilia's face around the corner. At this point, the massive shadow was no longer visible outside the window.

Togusa gazed out of the broken glass door and muttered the first thing that came to mind.

"...Well, the guy who actually owns this place is gone now, so how are we supposed to explain this if the cops show up?"

♂♀

In the dark of night, the shadow monster that was Celty Sturluson continued its chase of Kujiragi.

The woman leaped and bounded from rooftop to rooftop like she was going to cross a thousand leagues in the span of a night. Before the mass of shadow could fall, it extended tendrils of shadow that gripped buildings like some monstrous slime mold to keep itself aloft—yet the way it pursued Kujiragi was closer to a carnivorous beast on the hunt.

There was no end to the shadow tentacles. But those whiplike blades sliced through everything in their way.

Normally, if Celty had witnessed the bold act of warping Saika into other forms than a pure katana, she would have been alarmed, yet she would have watched carefully and calmly to formulate a proper response.

But in this state, she did not have that calm. She did not have any sense of reason whatsoever.

In fact, it was unclear whether the shadow monstrosity should even be referred to as "Celty Sturluson."

There wasn't a hint of Celty's consciousness in its actions, just an automated hunting system that pursued the fleeing Kujiragi.

Were the swarms of tendrils attempting to skewer Kujiragi's body, or were they trying to grab Shinra off her shoulder?

Kujiragi could not tell you the answer as she fled.

The shadow could not tell you the answer as it chased her.

Because the mass of shadow had eliminated the very sense of reason that would seek that answer in the first place.

♂♀

Shinra's apartment

"Nope, can't tell where they went."

Togusa and the others had stepped gingerly onto the veranda, avoiding the broken glass, but nowhere among the nearby buildings could they see the mysterious woman who'd abducted Shinra, or the freakish, monstrous form of Celty.

In the daytime would be one thing, but against the backdrop of night, it would be nearly impossible to see Celty in the sky.

"That chick with the glasses did that all in what, like, thirty seconds after entering the place? The hell is goin' on, man...," muttered Togusa, who was probably the most rational individual present.

And yet, thinking over what he had just seen, he came up with an answer to his own question that wasn't all that rational.

"Was it just me, or did that chick kinda look like Ruri?" He shook his head, dispelling the thought. "Nah...can't be."

As a matter of fact, Ruri Hijiribe and Kasane Kujiragi were niece and aunt, so he was actually entirely correct in his observation, but Togusa had no idea of that. He banished the thought and glanced over the railing of the balcony. "But what should we do about...?"

He didn't finish that sentence. It was interrupted by a braying that did not seem like anything from this world, coming from the bottom of the apartment building. It hit with the crackle and boom of a thunderbolt, echoing eerily throughout the night of the city.

Then, from the entrance to the basement parking garage, burst a shadowy black thing—not as big as what Togusa had seen moments earlier, but still significantly bigger than a human being. It reared up high among the streetlights. Togusa frowned and wondered, "Is that...a horse?"

It appeared to be a black creature with four distinctively long, narrow legs, but something about it still seemed to be weird and alien.

"Oh..."

A shiver ran down Togusa's back when he recognized that the source of his concern was the lack of a head on the creature. But by that point, the headless horse was already going down the alley, leaving behind only the echo of its rumbling cry into the night.

"What the hell is even happening, man...?"

He had thought he was used to Celty and the abnormality she represented. While he hadn't been as quick to embrace her as Yumasaki had been—and *he* was the one still jabbering on nearby—Togusa felt that he himself had accepted Celty and the fact that she was not human, but someone with whom you could have a relationship.

But the mass of shadow he had just witnessed made him realize that his take on the situation was naive.

"What the hell's even going on with the world...?" he wondered now. If it was at all something grandiose, it didn't feel like it to him.

Instead, his understanding of the world, as it appeared through his eyes, was being fundamentally overturned.

♂♀

Rooftop, parking garage, Tokyo

Several hours earlier, there was another person who, like Celty, had exploded with a potent cocktail of mixed emotions: the leader of the Yellow Scarves gang, Masaomi Kida.

A young man on edge, people liked to say.
It wasn't complimentary, but there was no other description that better captured what Masaomi was at this moment.

Just seconds before this, he had thrown himself into a tremendous fight.
You might say that Masaomi had cast his very life into challenging Chikage Rokujou, the leader of a motorcycle gang from Saitama—Chikage had superhuman toughness and strength, just not on the level of Shizuo Heiwajima. At the very least, Masaomi entered the fight with that expectation.
But in all accuracy, he did *not* cast his entire life into it, if you were to define that as fighting with the expectation of going up to and past the threshold of death. In fact, Masaomi was not thinking about dying in his fight against Chikage Rokujou.
Chikage's ferocious attacks.
The mad way that he leaped off the building, holding on to Masaomi.
On several occasions, Masaomi expected that death would result from these things. Yet, there was still a gap between what he experienced and the sense of impending death.
In large part, this was because he did not sense any murderous intent from Chikage Rokujou in their combat—but Masaomi was not able to perform this kind of subtle analysis in the moment.

*   *   *

No less than a minute before, Masaomi had seen Chikage Rokujou fall from the rooftop and be perfectly fine. Masaomi turned back to the roof so that he could regain control of the situation—and he witnessed another group of several dozen approaching who were very much not the Yellow Scarves.

And standing at the head of the group: a man with burn scars, holding a hard rubber hammer.

"Heh-hya...I guess it's true that idiots and smoke like to gather in high places, huh?"

Before his brain could process that voice, his very cells reacted.
The first memory that popped into his head was past terror.
Death.
This was the sense of certain impending doom.
If he went toward this man, he would be killed. His life would be erased. After he'd undergone suffering at the very limit of what he could fathom—if not even beyond it.
The memory of the first time he'd felt the powerful stench of death and fallen to his knees.
The moment he had abandoned the one person he must never abandon.

"*Here's your question!* When I broke Saki Mikajima's leg...who was the pussy who abandoned her and ran away?! Kee-hee-hya-ha-ha-ha-ha!"

And with those hideous, vexing words, Masaomi's entire world was shut in darkness.
Unlike with Celty, this was not a case of an emotional circuit breaker tripping.
In fact, it was almost the exact opposite of the change that would happen to her a few hours later.
When all of his emotions exploded, they switched *on* all the power lines that had been down inside Masaomi Kida.
Because he was human.
Because he could not get rid of his emotions.

Because he was dragging his past behind him.

His fear and anxiety all converted into rage, and he screamed the name of his opponent.

"Izumiiiiiii!"

He launched forward.

This time, he was truly putting his life on the line.

In that moment, the real determination to fight with his very life welled up from deep within. And at the same moment, it birthed another kind of determination.

When one offers up one's life, it is often life that is sought in return.

The sheer force of the powerful emotions raging within brought about a kind of secondary, imitation determination. He was prepared to kill the interloper, if need be. The difference in numbers was stark, and if anyone was going to end up dead here, Masaomi was by far the most likely.

But still he ran.

Not like a man with tunnel vision.

He saw the obvious suffering ahead of him and chose to throw all his rising emotions into overcoming it.

Masaomi was not a very tall man. He was used to fighting, and he had a pretty decent physical build, but he didn't cut the sort of figure that struck fear into others with a glance.

But he *did* cast off a demonic fury that was unlike your typical teenager, and it caused the thugs around him to subconsciously shy away a bit.

In their midst, the very source of Masaomi's nightmares, Ran Izumii, smirked at his foe through sunglasses and raised his hammer.

"...You mean *Mr.* Izumii, yeah?"

And just like that, he swung it down at Masaomi's head.

Masaomi avoided the swing by a hair's width, putting him right inside his opponent's defenses.

"_____"

There was nothing to say.

As if to make the point that nothing could be worth saying to this man, no words of hatred even being worth the effort, Masaomi put all the strength and emotion he could summon, all the regrets about his own weakness, and every other thing that had built up inside him into a clenched fist.

He twisted his body, putting rotation into the greatest possible blow he could muster, and then tensed and paused for an instant.

Just the slightest, briefest moment.

It was enough time for Izumii to recognize Masaomi's stance and the distance between them and hastily attempt to evade. But rolling his upper half backward did not create enough room to avoid impact.

Masaomi's fist hurtled with maximum speed and weight at Izumii's unprotected face.

The next moment, the sound of violent impact echoed off the walls of the parking garage.

♂♀

In the past

Ran Izumii was once the head of the Blue Squares, but he was not the kind of person you would consider a mighty brawler.

For one thing, he got the position only because it was left to him by his little brother, Aoba Kuronuma. So in the sense that he was never meant to earn that leadership position, it was true—because he *didn't* build that throne for himself.

However, it was under Izumii's lead that the Blue Squares actually expanded their power. So it was more accurate to describe him as a true scumbag.

He relied on numbers in battle, and out of an inferiority complex to his popular and charismatic brother, he tended to try to keep people under control with fear instead.

He would focus on annihilating enemy gangs, keeping them under his thumb with violence, and using his followers as the limbs that did his bidding. Kadota criticized him for his methods on many an occasion, but Izumii never intended to take that into account.

He knew that if he stopped growing the Blue Squares his brother had built and he allowed it to be comfortable in its own skin, it was bound to implode instead. And once that happened, *he* would be the first one its members turned against.

So he committed himself to atrocity: He wielded violence like a cudgel. He indulged in all his desires. He painted the back alleys of Ikebukuro in sticky, ugly fear, grinding the city rough and raw.

Because as soon as he stopped, that fear would crush him in return.

On the other hand, Ran Izumii was not some victim whose life had been sent off the rails by his brother's actions. While he was unable to stop the relentless march of his gang, it was also by his own desire that he traced this path.

If he were really some sympathetic victim, he would have handed the gang over to someone else, retired from the position, and left the ugly, bloodstained back alleys behind.

In fact, if he had left it in the hands of Kadota, for example, the team might have come together well. A guy like him had the potential and the character to lead. He might even have altered the fundamental nature of the gang.

But Izumii refused to do that.

The power and money and influence he gained were all *his*, and the thought of giving them up to another person was unfathomable. Izumii was steering them down the path of madness because he wanted to do it.

In other words, he was a real scumbag.

But there were dangerous storm clouds around his path.

There was a street gang, supposedly set up by middle school kids, that wore yellow bandannas. This group, the Yellow Scarves, was somehow holding its own against the Blue Squares' overwhelming advantage in numbers.

This inexplicable situation did not stop Izumii. When their relentless guerrilla assaults were proving to be impossible to overcome with his power of numbers, he began to get impatient—until a certain man made unexpected contact with him and gave Izumii some information.

That the leader of the Yellow Scarves was Masaomi Kida.

And that he had a girlfriend by the name of Saki Mikajima.
And how they could get her alone.

Izumii didn't trust him, but he was willing to take any help he could get and accepted the man's offer. They succeeded in kidnapping the girl, and all they needed to do after that was use her to lure Masaomi Kida to a place where they could crush him.

But as a result, Izumii lost his status, his power, and even the tiny bit of freedom he possessed. All he gained was the facial-burn scar from Yumasaki's Molotov cocktail.

Izumii benefited from not having a significant prior arrest record, but he was still sentenced for his assault, and he spent time in juvenile detention.

While he served his sentence, he coincidentally learned about the trickery involved in the warfare between the Blue Squares and Yellow Scarves. That he had been placed on his throne by his brother and manipulated in the palm of a man named Izaya Orihara, who wanted to throw a wrench into the gang war.

At last, Izumii understood just how powerless he really was.

If he was the type of person to learn humility, his story would likely have taken a different route at this point.

But he was not.

He was not meant to inspire others with leadership, but he was indeed a bona fide scumbag.

Not for a single second did the emptiness consume him. Rather than reflect on his failings or look ahead to his future, he simply doubled down on the simmering, obsessive hatred within him.

He didn't think he'd done anything wrong.

So Izumii punched the wall of the facility's gym. He kicked it, screamed, and even head-butted the hard surface. It was identified as self-harming behavior, and he was placed in a solitary cell.

But he wasn't trying to hurt himself at all—Izumii just wanted to destroy something, anything, that was within reach.

Since he wasn't Shizuo Heiwajima, he did not destroy the prison wall, of course. His limbs did not break and heal again with super-human speed, like Shizuo's.

Instead, Izumii became a quiet, model inmate from that point on. He kept the fury and hatred he felt for the world suppressed deep down, so that they seeped into each and every cell of his being.

Izumii didn't engage in any special training. There was no human drama that changed his outlook on life, and he did not gain any super-human powers. He just quietly served out his sentence.

But there was a slight change in him.

That is, if you can call erasing something that was once within him a "change."

All he did was extend the one remarkable characteristic he possessed.

Toward the act of destruction, *he no longer felt any hesitation at all*.

In other words, he no longer had any kind of braking mechanism to prevent him from engaging in destruction.

He didn't care about destroying his own body.

He didn't think about the risk of going back to prison.

He didn't consider the danger that someone might lose their life.

Ran Izumii simply dedicated himself to destroying.

Not in spontaneous bursts of anger, as Shizuo Heiwajima did—but with the full variety of all kinds of hatred that he harbored within himself.

He could swing that hammer of destruction at anyone and anything. That's all he did.

♂♀

Present day, parking garage

Time passed, and at last, Ran Izumii and Masaomi Kida came face-to-face in violent conflict.

*   *   *

Red blood dripped to the ground between the two, accompanied by the sound of bone cracking. Izumii and Masaomi paused in the moment of connection between fist and head.

This frozen moment made one thing clear.

It was that Masaomi had thrown a straight right powerful enough to damage the bones of the neck—and that Izumii's body did not fly off its feet from the impact.

"…"

It was Masaomi who winced from the pain.

His fist did indeed make contact with Izumii's head. But it was not direct to the face; rather, it was above the forehead, near his crown. Izumii had been bending backward, seemingly to avoid the punch, but now his torso was leaning forward.

The bending *wasn't* to avoid the punch; it was so that he could head-butt Masaomi's fist. Izumii had swung his upper half around like a spring, striking Masaomi's punch with the top of his head.

It broke Masaomi's fist and sent blood dripping from his lacerated flesh. Even the injuries to his fingers looked worse than simple fractures or dislocations.

Paralysis instantly turned to heat, and heat instantly turned to pain, which shot through his spine, amplifying into agony.

But while Masaomi winced at the pain, the strength did not leave his eyes and mouth. Izumii leered at him, earning a fierce glare in response, and asked in a rasping voice, "Did you think…I would be a pushover?"

Masaomi didn't answer. He pulled his fist away and leaped off the ground, intending to drive his knee directly into Izumii's downturned face.

But this move was already anticipated. The hammer came flying in from a blind angle and struck the cap of Masaomi's knee.

"…!"

The hammer blow broke the patella, and Masaomi's kick hit nothing but air.

He tried to land on his feet, but the pain in his knee caused him to topple over. As Masaomi lay on the ground, Izumii leered over him.

"Did you think that because I have all these thugs following me, I was the kind of wuss who needed them to do all my dirty work?"

He promptly kicked Masaomi to punctuate his sentiment. The boy, prone on the ground, turned on his side and crossed his arms to absorb the blow.

But Izumii's kick was too strong. He could hear his arm bones cracking, and more blood flew from his crushed fist.

If he'd turned the other way to show his back, it might have caused less damage. But Masaomi's emotions were at such a high that he refused to do so—and for two different reasons.

One, because he sensed that taking his eyes off the man for any reason would be extremely perilous; and two, because he felt that he could never show his back to *this man* again in his life.

"Izumii...," Masaomi groaned, leveling an extraordinary amount of loathing through his eyes. The man just laughed it off.

"Did you think I was no better than Horada at this, Masaomi Kidaaa?"

"..."

"Did you think that acting like the tragic hero and letting the adrenaline take over was gonna do the trick to get you over the hump? Nah, the tragic part is that you earned all of this yourself! Hya-ha-ha-ha!"

"Shut up...," Masaomi grunted, getting to his feet despite the pain in his knee—if he even felt it at all.

Izumii threw his hands wide and shouted, "And now, your question!"

The other thugs around him began to stir on that cue. The circle surrounding him broke, but only to bring a new fact to light.

"If you don't let me kill you right here and now, what's going to happen to your beloved little shitheads, hmm?"

Masaomi was looking at his fellow Yellow Scarves, who had been on the rooftop all along. Now each one of them was subdued by at least two of Izumii's goons and unable to do anything.

"You bastard!" he swore, eyes filling with even more hatred and rage.

But like Izumii was hoping, Masaomi did stand down at this point. One of his followers called out in a tremulous voice, "Sh-Shogun! Forget about us! Just get outta here!"

Izumii turned slowly to face the one who'd spoken up. "Ooh, very cool. So you're a tragic hero, too, huh?" He tossed his hammer back and forth from hand to hand, strolling casually toward the captured boy. "Let me guess… You think you're safe from bein' killed over some stupid fight between kids?"

"Knock it off!" Masaomi shouted, trying to bolt forward, but his leg gave way, and he fell to his knees again.

"It's because it's a stupid fight between kids that you're gonna die just like that. Moron." Izumii gleefully clenched the hammer in his right hand and lifted his arm up high.

"Stop it, Izumii!" the Yellow Scarves leader yelled, part rage and part plea. "If you're gonna kill anyone, kill me! They're not part of this!"

Izumii paused and turned back. "Not part of this? They're wearing your yellow bandannas, and you wanna claim they have nothing to do with you? Is that right?" He chuckled and traced his burn scar with a finger. "Well, the answer to the quiz I just gave you was 'They're gonna die either way'! Hya-ha-ha-ha! Why would I ever let any of the Yellow Scarves get off easy?!"

"Because…they don't have anything to do with me and you!"

The fact that there were hostages was like cold water poured over Masaomi's boiling emotions, allowing rationale to make its way into his head.

Now that they were having an actual dialogue, Izumii rolled his neck, popping the vertebrae, and let the corners of his mouth curl upward in delight.

"Yeah. You're right, huh? I personally don't got nothin' to do with these small-time Yellow Scarves, I suppose. And the score I got to settle with you ain't nothin' to talk about compared with guys like Kadota and Yumasaki."

"In that case—!"

"But the thing is…I'm in the Dollars, see? And once I come across our rival group, I got an obligation to destroy 'em…"

Dollars.

The mention of the word was even icier water over Masaomi's mind. Unease and fear grew within him to balance out his raging fury.

Izumii spun the hammer between his fingers. "If I don't, then I got to *answer to our boss, Ryuugamine,* don't I?"

*   *   *

The word *boss* was delivered with mockery that lacked even a shred of respect.

And yet, the mention of the name threw a number of reflexive emotional switches inside Masaomi.

"What...did you...just say?" he demanded, getting unsteadily to his feet. But while his voice was thick with anger, there was also a note of pleading, of hoping that he had somehow heard something wrong.

Izumii grinned sadistically, perhaps picking up on this, and rapped the end of the hammer against his own shoulder. "Mikado Ryuugamine, our leader. What's it to ya?"

"He's not—!"

"What about him?"

"...!" The right answer didn't immediately pop into Masaomi's head.

Izumii cackled. "What's wrong? What're you so scared of? You knew this already, didn't cha? It's why you came back to play the big boy and lead the Yellow Scarves again, yeah? So you could pick this fight?" He cracked his neck again and spat. "With us Dollars?"

"You're...Dollars?"

"Yeah, what's your problem? Thanks to Kadota and y'all, my gang broke up, remember? So here I am, rising up the ranks from the bottom, like a dedicated worker should. I think I deserve props for that," Izumii mocked.

But it was no joke to Masaomi. Was the cold sweat running down his cheeks from the pain in his hand and knee, or was it more of a mental thing?

"What are you going to do...to Mikado?"

"*Do?* Dunno. I never met the guy in person. But from what I hear, I don't even need to do nothin' to him. He's hauled off and gone crazy on his own."

"Oh, screw you... What would you know about him—?"

"What would I know? I don't know *shit*, dumb-ass!"

Izumii's kick caught Masaomi on the shoulder. He lost his balance and fell over. Izumii stomped on him and continued, "Now, your question! If you know everything about your buddy, then surely you can tell me why Mr. Ryuugamine has lost his mind! And whose fault is it that your friends over there are going to get destroyed, and whose fault is it that your precious girlfriend's legs got broken...?"

He paused, smirking gleefully. When Masaomi only glared back without a word, he raised his hammer again.

"The answer is…obviously, every last bit of it is your fault, moron!"

And he swung it downward, no hesitation, toward Masaomi and his gritted teeth.

But…

"That's enough of that."

…a hand grabbed Izumii's wrist just below where he held the hammer.

"…Wha…?" He glared through his shades at this interruption.

It was a man, standing right behind him.

"Hang on… Aren't you the guy who was fightin' with this kid just now?"

"Well, seems you're already caught up on the situation."

The men around Chikage Rokujou buzzed and murmured. He had stridden through their circle so boldly, they initially assumed that he was just another member of the group.

"Don't step in and steal my opponent," Rokujou stated.

Izumii scowled and asked, "Didn't you just fall off the edge over there?" jutting his chin toward the side of the rooftop.

"Yeah, I did," he admitted.

"So why didn't you just die?"

Izumii sent a signal to the rest of his thugs with a glance. A number of them grinned and laid hands on Rokujou's shoulders. "What do you think you're doing, bud…? *Ngwah?!*"

"Sorry. I'm not into guys just touching me out of nowhere," said Rokujou. He had struck the face of one of the punks behind him with a backhand, giving him a bloody nose.

"You son of a…"

A different thug tried to hit him, but Rokujou grabbed him by the face first. He had the guy firmly around the head, thumb pressed right over his eyelid. When the thug realized that the fate of his eyeball depended on the whim of his opponent, he tensed, unable to strike back.

"All right, fellas, nobody's gonna move now, okay? Not unless you wanna see your buddy's eyeball explode." Rokujou maintained his grip on the guy's face but let go of Izumii's arm and leaned back against a nearby pillar.

"...Are you insane?" said Izumii.

Rokujou gave him a breezy glance.

"A lot saner than you, I bet."

"..."

All of this brought Masaomi back to reality. The series of cold showers he'd just taken snapped his mind to attention and helped him realize he'd just been saved by the guy he was fighting not long ago—and made him remember just where he was.

But all of it was too late.

Then again, with this many opponents, would it have even mattered whether he'd been thinking straight? At the very least, he might have been able to run away. But in that case, what would have happened to his companions?

They were screwed from the moment the other group showed up.

Masaomi actually felt a painful sense of regret that his own lack of caution had gotten Rokujou involved in something unnecessary—a remarkable bit of empathy for the man he'd practically been trying to kill minutes before.

It's just not going to work out. Not against this many... Not unless I was Shizuo Heiwajima.

Why was he so weak?

Was this just going to be a repeat of the past?

But Masaomi tried to stand, weathering these self-doubts and more. He wasn't going to be satisfied until he at least punched this guy's lights out. Hatred for Izumii bristled through Masaomi, and the emotion erased the pain of his wounds.

But before he could stand, Rokujou interjected.

"Listen, are you folks all right in the head? I realize I was just fighting with this guy minutes ago, but you do know that if you kill him, the security cameras are gonna get y'all arrested, right?"

"What? You... You don't think *that's* gonna frighten us, do ya?" Izumii drawled, his shoulders shaking with laughter. "You think we're stupid enough not to cut off the power to the cameras? In the time it'll take a technician to come out and check on it, it ain't no thing to pulverize the whole lotta you."

It seemed like mere mockery, but Masaomi and the Yellow Scarves could sense that when he said "pulverize," Izumii wasn't just talking about beating them up. He was not making a threat or playing a mind game, but stating a fact.

· "Yeah, I see what you mean," Rokujou said. "Myself aside, that guy on the floor over there and the ones you've caught here are gonna die."

"And so will you," Izumii growled.

Rokujou ignored him and sighed. "Oh, bother. Sometimes you get stand-up guys like Kadota, and sometimes you get real trash like you folks. I swear, I just can't figure out this Dollars group."

"…Did you say Kadota?"

"You know him? He's several levels above you in character. But you probably already know that, right?"

"…"

The smile vanished from Izumii's face. His teeth ground audibly. Then he looked at the man whose face Rokujou was still holding, and he said, "You can take his eye."

"I-Izumii?!" the thug shrieked, but Izumii wasn't listening anymore.

"But you're going to die here for it."

"So I get to take one eye, and it costs me my life? What kind of rip-off are you running here?" Rokujou wondered with a wry shrug.

"If you get ripped off, it's because you were stupid," Izumi muttered simply. He raised his hand and started giving an order to the hoodlums around him. "Forget it. Turn this guy to dust—"

He did not finish his sentence.

Rokujou released the man he was grabbing—and ducked around the back side of the pillar.

"Hey, c'mon, you don't think you can get away from…," Izumii started to say, but then he noticed the bit of red sticking out from behind the pillar.

The moment Rokujou started doing whatever it was he was doing behind the pillar, a number of the thugs who could see it from that angle started to look panicked.

"Stop him!" he yelled, but it was too late.

Rokujou pressed the object that was attached to the other side of the pillar: an emergency fire alarm.

The alarm began blaring and rattling. People walking around on the street near the parking garage stopped and stared.

Even the office workers from adjacent buildings still at their jobs peered out to see what the matter was. All of a sudden, the completely ordinary parking garage that melted into the background was now a focal point of the city.

"You've gotta be an idiot to destroy only the cameras," Rokujou muttered, though his words were drowned out by the alarm and never reached his opponent's ears.

But Izumii could tell he was being insulted, and his eyes flashed with fury as they focused on Rokujou. "You… You're mocking me, aren't you…?"

He looked so furious that he might have launched himself at once, but he held back, sensing that the destruction he hoped to wreak could no longer be achieved. Instead, he gritted his teeth and sent a hand signal to his followers.

But a number of the thugs had already fled the garage due to the fire alarm, and in the confusion, the Yellow Scarves held captive had the opportunity to gain their freedom. They rushed over to Masaomi at once and began pulling him away from Izumii.

"You…little…fuckers…"

Knowing Izumii's personality, this was exactly the moment he would chase down Masaomi to deliver a decisive blow—but for some reason, he was just standing there, sweating profusely, his face twitching.

It was the sound of the alarm, dredging up the trauma of his immolation at Yumasaki's hands.

"C'mon, Izumii, let's go! The cops are gonna show up!" one of his companions yelled into his ear.

"Tsk… Lucky bastard." Spitting the words out, he shoved down the unsettling fear in his heart and headed to the exit with his team.

He did turn back one last time to look at Rokujou with loathing and say, "I'm gonna remember you…"

But when he actually faced that direction, two shadows crossed his vision.

They were the soles of Rokujou's shoes.

Both his right foot and his left lined up for a beauty of a dropkick.

Before Izumii could register what was happening, they struck him square in the chest—and he rocketed and tumbled backward a good thirty feet, his sternum cracking under the sheer force of the blow.

A number of the hoodlums lifted up the unconscious Izumii.

"At least kill *him*, dammit!"

About ten of the feistier thugs turned to Rokujou, holding metal pipes and knives and such.

"Listen... I'd love to spend time with you, but I'm not waitin' for the police." Rokujou turned on his heel and rushed over to the Yellow Scarves who were dragging Masaomi away. "You guys should clear out, too. Don't get caught, okay?"

"Huh? H-hey, wait...," they murmured, but Rokujou just grabbed Masaomi and lifted him up.

"...Ah?" Masaomi was conscious enough to be taken by surprise, even through the incredible pain.

"Easier to get away if I'm the one carrying you than those guys, eh? We can continue our fight some other time."

Thanks to the alarm making it harder to hear, the other Yellow Scarves couldn't tell what was going on, and they tried to stop Rokujou from rushing away with Masaomi over his shoulder.

"Wh-what are you saying...? Ah! Hey!"

Rokujou ignored them and, using a car parked next to the fence around the rooftop as a stepping stone, leaped right over the wall.

"Hey, that can't be—! Are you serious—? What the hell?!" the boys shouted all at once, to the sound of Masaomi's yelp.

But Rokujou just jumped right off the edge without a second's hesitation.

"Whoaaaaaa?!"

It was so sudden, so startling, that Masaomi actually forgot his pain for a moment.

The impact was far softer than he'd expected, and he realized that some of the energy of their fall was being directed sideways. Through bouncing, blurry vision, he could see a streetlight swaying.

Apparently, Rokujou had used the streetlight as a landing pad. And in the next moment, there was a dull *thwump*, and Masaomi felt their momentum changing directions again.

"...Huh?"

First he confirmed that he was still alive, and then the agony of his fist and knee injuries flooded back. He looked around, trying to withstand the pain, and saw that the scenery around him was moving. Then his body landed on a rough, woven surface.

"Yeow..."

"Sorry about that. Just stay down for a bit. If the cops find us, they'll put a stop to it all."

He recognized that his body was resting on the top of a covered truck. Overhead, the thugs were staring dumbfoundedly down at them from the roof level of the parking garage. Some of them were even beating on the chain-link fence in frustration. Given that none of the faces he could see belonged to the Yellow Scarves, Masaomi surmised that they must have run off as soon as they saw he was safely on the ground.

Masaomi looked at the sky, praying that they got away without trouble, and said, "Am... Am I alive?"

"Better thank me. If the cops or Dollars catch you, you're not gettin' away on that leg," Rokujou said with a grin. The scenery sped by behind him as the truck picked up velocity.

Masaomi glanced back at the garage vanishing into the distance and asked:

"So what happens now?"

♂♀

Several hours later, parking garage

"Buncha kids gettin' up to no good again," muttered one of the police officers patrolling the roof of the parking garage. They'd come here because an incident had happened earlier in the day.

The entire area was on heightened alert, due to an attack on a police vehicle about an hour ago. There hadn't been any trouble at this structure recently, but there was a report about a fire alarm going off, and many young ruffians were witnessed around it. The power line to the security cameras had also been cut.

Given the timing of the other incident, the orders went out to strengthen local patrols to check out the garage, even if it was unlikely that the events were connected.

"You know about the period when the street gangs used to use this place as a hideout, Mr. Kuzuhara?" asked a younger officer.

Ginichirou Kuzuhara, a man entering middle age, sighed and said, "I do. You're new on this beat, so you don't know, but they used to fight all the time at this garage. It stopped cold about two years back...but ever since that incident with the street slasher, there's just been a bad vibe around."

"Doesn't help when you've got that freaky Headless Rider putting on a public performance," said the younger cop. He hadn't seen the rider much, and he seemed to think it was just some kind of outlaw biker who liked to do circus tricks.

Ginichirou, however, had been around for years, and he remembered when the Headless Rider had first come to this city. He scowled and said, "Mmm...well, listen. There's stuff in this world that doesn't make logical sense. If that rider were a simple street performer, Kinnosuke would have had 'em lassoed up long ago." The name he'd dropped was that of his own blood relation, a traffic officer who rode a motorcycle of his own.

The rookie laughed. "Oh, geez, are you trying to tell me the Headless Rider really is some kind of monster? It's just a magic trick. Sleight of hand."

"...Turning your motorcycle into a horse?"

"Yeah. Don't you keep up with magicians, Mr. Kuzuhara? Over in America, they can make huge things disappear, like the Statue of Liberty and high-rise buildings and stuff! Even in Japan, we've got guys who can make frogs appear in their empty hands!"

"...Uh-huh." Ginichirou looked at his partner with something akin to pity. "Well, I guess that's better than getting all freaked out about it..."

"What was that, sir?"

"Just watch yourself for scams, kid."

"Oh, geez, Mr. Kuzuhara, you're the one who's convinced of occult answers for everything!" returned his partner at a chatter.

The full tour of the structure turned up nothing out of order. They finished examining the camera vandalization and, finding no reason to stick around, headed quickly for the next spot on their patrol.

But then an odd sound from the northwest caught their attention.

"…What was that?"

The younger officer returned to the roof level to look in the direction of the sound. What he witnessed there was quite eerie.

Heading from rooftop to rooftop, and sometimes lodging itself into the sides of buildings, was a figure carrying something large, swinging and leaping about like an American comic book hero with a spider motif.

Chasing after this figure was a black cloud—or a *thing* in cloud form. It was hard to tell against the night sky, but something black was there, absorbing all the light that hit it.

Occasionally, some black feelers would extend from *the thing*, and the figure would use some narrow silver object to swipe and cut at them to keep them away. The strange sound they heard was revealed to be the sound of the silver and black objects making contact.

Sometimes the black shadow would stop sending its tendrils forward, instead forming huge fangs that bit and lunged at the human figure. But the figure would leap with speed and agility to evade attack. It reminded the young officer of an action game he had played on his last day off.

"…Huh? No, wait, wait, wait."

He came to his senses, pressed himself harder against the fence, and stared. But by that point, the shapes were gone, having passed behind buildings between him and them.

"What's up? What was that sound?" said Ginichirou, walking up from behind.

The young officer rubbed his eyes near the bridge of his nose and said, as much to himself as to his partner, "It was…a street magician."

"A street magician…? You need a break. You're obsessed."

"No, I am not possessed! Don't try to scare me, sir!"

"...?"

♂♀

Ginichirou was becoming concerned for the rookie's mental health, but in the meantime, the actual source of the sound, the chase between Kasane Kujiragi and the black mass, continued.

"...It's time," Kujiragi muttered and made a sharp change of direction with Shinra over her shoulder. For just a moment as she leaped between buildings, she looked backward and drew a number of pen-like objects from her waist.

She gathered up the cylindrical objects and nimbly hurled them at the mass of shadow. It continued rushing for her, completely ignoring the projectiles. But Kujiragi looked forward again and resumed her jumping.

The next moment, the special pen-shaped flashbangs burst all at once, dazzling a small part of Ikebukuro briefly amid the darkness of night.

For a moment—just a moment—the flash caused the shadow creature to falter.

An ordinary human being would have been blinded and immobilized, but Celty did not have eyes to begin with, and her sense of vision recovered from flashes of light much faster—although this was only for her rational, humanoid form, not whatever she had become now.

But for that one brief moment, there was the possibility that she had lost her sight.

Celty knew this because Kujiragi then vanished from the rooftop, and her mass of shadow lost sense of where to go next for several seconds.

But seconds were merely seconds. It launched back into motion, perhaps sensing the alien power of Saika's body, and hurtled itself toward the gap between two particular buildings.

There, it found Kujiragi, who had deftly descended the wall of the building. She was in an alley down below, far from the shopping district, and there were no people around.

But with its special type of vision, the shadow mass saw Kujiragi lowering Shinra from her shoulder to the arms of *someone else*.

There was a car parked on the street at the entrance to the alley, and next to it, a human being who was helping Kujiragi load Shinra into it.

The instant it saw this, the shadow creature stopped again.

Kujiragi rushed farther down the alley. The car began to drive, pulling away in the other direction.

Until this point, there had been only one target. But now there were two going opposite ways.

One was the woman named Kujiragi, who'd hurt and stolen the shadow's beloved.

The other was that beloved, Shinra Kishitani—now captive to Saika's curse.

Hatred or love?

It was a simple set of options.

As a monster of sheer instinct and no reason, Celty finally displayed hesitation.

But it was not the return of sanity. If that were true, she would have decided, "First thing is to confirm that Shinra is safe, and then I can hunt down the woman."

No, in this situation, that emotional circuit breaker was still tripped. She was virtually unconscious of anything she was doing.

Yet, thirst does not require conscious will to desire water.

A moth does not require conscious will to fly toward the fire.

Whatever existed in the boundary between instinct and reason for her was being tested in this moment.

And then Celty, in her inhuman, freakish form, made her choice.

The shadowy mass plunged and writhed toward the vehicle carrying Shinra. Whether this was merely a coin flip or a conscious decision that she would have made every single time, it was impossible to know.

But Kujiragi decided that it was the latter. She watched the creature go, narrowing her eyes slightly, and muttered, "So even in this situation, you choose something else...over destruction and hatred."

She recalled a past crime she had committed: upon Ruri Hijiribe, the girl who shared her blood but was treated like a human, and who had nearly gained human happiness because of it.

Kujiragi recalled what she had done to her, and the flow of emotions that had transpired. "I'm afraid I must admit," she said, a tiny flash of danger crossing her lifeless robotic features, "that I was *jealous* of you."

Then ten finger blades, five from each hand, extended over the alley like steel wires. They bit into the walls of buildings on either side, bouncing off and stretching farther. The swarm of Saikas writhed like living creatures into abstract patterns.

The Saikas stretched and crossed like fine netting, blocking the path of Celty's monstrous form. But she charged straight ahead, seemingly unconcerned—until solid shadow and Saika's blades smashed together, sending sparks and shadow alike about the area.

The two inhuman things ground and scraped against each other. While the alley was desolately empty, the sound was tremendous, and those who happened to be close enough to hear it assumed it was probably the death cry of a bird or something—such was the ability of this particular sound to set the human mind on edge.

Monstrous Celty attempted to force her way through the net of metal, but only because she was singularly direct in her pursuit of the car with Shinra inside.

Narrowing the shadow to pass through the smaller spaces, attacking Kujiragi directly, or simply pulling back and making her way around her—all of these were simple ideas, the kind a monkey or a dog would quickly attempt. Something even the smallest amount of rational thinking would produce, and yet she did not.

She was so absent of any critical thought at the moment that her only action was to pursue one person: Shinra Kishitani, the man who had given her a place in the human world.

♂♀

The vehicle rushed away from Kujiragi. On the floor beneath the back seat was a man dressed in pajamas that resembled a lab coat.

His eyes were red and bloodshot, and his vision was woozy. Shinra Kishitani was a pitiable victim, a "child" implanted with the curse of Saika's love.

Through Saika, Kujiragi had ordered him to stay put and behave for a while. Knowing that she needed to abduct him, she probably figured that if he put up a fight, it would cause trouble.

So as ordered, Shinra did not struggle at all throughout his captivity and was still under her control, awaiting further orders.

And yet—when the rattling, scraping bird death cry from the distant alley reached the car, his lips curved into a tiny smile. With bloodshot eyes and a smile on his face, he murmured to himself:

"Ha-ha...a fool...hardy...charge...indeed..."

♂♀

Driver's seat

Only one person heard Shinra mutter.

It was the person who'd been hired to take him from Kujiragi and drive him to a specified location.

"..."

She considered the potential meaning of his words, but Vorona, the mercenary behind the wheel, decided he was simply delirious from fever, and she did not spend any more time thinking about it.

What am I being forced to ferry right now?

She was currently working for Kujiragi, who had been Jinnai Yodogiri's secretary. It wasn't clear why Kujiragi, rather than Yodogiri, had come to hire Vorona, but the jobs themselves were taking her into more dangerous territory than Yodogiri's had.

One was stealing a silver case from a police vehicle—an act of war against the national power of Japan. The second was kidnapping someone and running from a monster.

She had a decent idea of what the group of shadows trying to rush after her vehicle from the alley actually was. If Slon were present, he would warn her that it was dangerous to make an enemy of monsters. But her partner was no longer here to apply the brakes.

His eyes looked very bloodshot to me. Was he infected by some kind of virus, perhaps? she wondered briefly, alarmed, but given that her client had carried the man over her shoulder, Vorona banished the possibility from her mind.

If Slon were here, he might say something like "Wait, I'm suspicious. What if the client already took a vaccine for it? Now I can't sleep at night."

But there was no one with Vorona now.

No one at her side.

It filled Vorona with an odd feeling of loneliness. She had done a number of jobs by herself already. But because they'd been so cut-and-dried, she hadn't had time to view them as particularly solitary.

But the reason she was feeling especially lonely now was the thought of another person who ought to be with her. A person who was not Slon.

The first temporary job she'd taken in Japan to make ends meet was at a debt-collection business. It was the kind of place that operated just on the dark side of the gray zone, but that didn't matter to Vorona, who was used to utterly criminal work.

And what she found there was an interpersonal relationship different from what she had with Slon.

Shizuo Heiwajima was a man she had once tried to kill, a man she had failed to destroy, and a man who had obliterated Vorona's own value system.

As she had spent time with their boss, Tom, as well as the other people at the company, Vorona had come to form a strong connection to a world she had never known before—a world she'd been introduced to for the very first time through Shizuo.

Vorona had never loved a human being before. She probably didn't even love herself.

She knew of love only as a piece of discrete knowledge. She couldn't decide whether the thing called love was something her life needed or not.

Beyond understanding the concept, she had never actually experienced the emotion of love.

That was no different now. But there was something she had learned in place of love.

The sufficiency and satisfaction of living itself, or in other words, peace.

Until this point, any day in which nothing wild happened was a day she might as well not have lived at all. She wanted to offer up her life as a prize, to wager it against the existence of the mighty. That moment of destroying a powerful opponent was the moment she felt she was truly living.

But the thirst, the drive that caused her heart and mind to creak, was completely gone. She did not feel it, and in fact, she hadn't even noticed it was gone until she was reunited with Slon, whom she'd thought dead, and he pronounced that she had grown "tepid."

That wasn't the biggest shock, however. It was that despite denying it at that time, deep in her heart, she realized she had thought, *That might not be so bad, actually.*

Vorona had tried to cut off that thought at the root, but Izaya Orihara sneaked past her mental defenses and poured poison into her mind.

The poison slowly but surely spread, eating away at her and replaying memory after memory of humiliation. When this coincided with Shizuo's arrest, she began to regain her old self bit by bit, and now she was doing jobs for Kujiragi.

When she attacked the police vehicle, she might not have killed the person driving it, but she certainly did enough to regain that sense of elation in pursuing only strength.

And then something happened right after that to completely dash her high.

"Hey, is that...*Vorona*?"

Shizuo Heiwajima just so happened to be there. When he recognized her, Vorona felt that all time in the world had briefly frozen.

She didn't know why she'd felt that way. But she remembered that she'd experienced a sudden flood of despair, fear, and unease.

She'd said nothing to Shizuo, trying to stifle that feeling, and left the scene without a word.

There was nothing else she could do.

*   *   *

And in the time from then to now, through a sensation of unfathomable loss, she finally understood what her own emotions were.

Like Slon had said, she'd been affected by this country, colored by it. She'd spent a very different kind of time with Shizuo Heiwajima, the man she'd sworn to destroy. And in a period of peace and safety, without risking her life, she found a different kind of happiness from the kind she received when attempting to kill the mighty.

It makes sense to me. I'm afraid. Afraid of losing what I have now.

But as she performed Kujiragi's jobs, she realized that risking her life to fight powerful foes and putting herself in danger gave her a particular kind of joy of its own.

By reconfirming what she knew about herself, Vorona came to a certain opinion: She did not have the right to live in a peaceful country like this, surrounded by the bliss and warmth it offered her.

I think...maybe the period when I was working with Father might have been the best time of my life.

She was flooded with alternating hatred and nostalgia when she thought about her father, an officer in an arms-trading company.

She couldn't just toss everything out. She couldn't make it that simple.

What about her was actually strong?

Did she really have the right to fight against powerful opponents at all?

At this late stage, Vorona began to question her own self. But there was no stopping her present course.

Now that Shizuo Heiwajima knew what she was, the peaceful life she might have enjoyed was gone forever.

Meanwhile, Vorona, too, could hear the eerie creaking of collisions between inhuman creatures. In the rearview mirror, she could see a writhing shadow in the street, but it was lost in the night as she pulled away from it.

Once around the corner, where she could no longer see the shadow, Vorona thought to herself, *Are monsters now prowling the streets regularly? What is becoming of the world? I bet President Lingerin would enjoy this situation, however.*

It seemed as though the city was plunging into chaos, but something about it was familiar, nostalgic. It reminded her of the past.

But even she knew that this was just her own mind trying to escape its present problem.

And she noted, with some loneliness, that there was no Shizuo Heiwajima in those old memories of hers.

♂♀

At that moment, Ikebukuro

Shizuo Heiwajima was irritated.

"Hey, yo! Old man, I know you! You that Shizuo Heiwajima? The real deal?"

"That bartender look sticks out. You think that looks good on you, huh? You pullin' that off?"

It was a much less crowded area, a good distance away from the main shopping district. Shizuo was out of police custody now and surrounded by a group of young men who were not the brightest of the bunch.

"You're famous, yeah? I bet you make bank, bro! You could give us some allowance, I bet."

"Why don't you *say somethin'*, old man?!"

There were three accosting him at the moment, but including the ones grinning at him from a distance, the total size of the group was closer to ten.

He didn't recognize any of them from around town. Given that they were all on bikes, they could even be middle school students. Most likely they were using the summer vacation time to come out and visit from a distant neighboring city, like Saitama.

"…Get lost," he muttered, clicking his tongue with ever greater irritation.

This isn't it. Neither that fleabrain nor the red-eyed guys would send punks like this after me.

His irritation was not at this lazy attempt to intimidate him, but at the fact that it wasn't what he'd expected to see.

It wasn't clear why Vorona would be doing this. But he could assume she was tangled up in something involving either a pawn of the detestable Izaya Orihara or someone related to that cursed sword.

Even if Vorona's actions were totally unrelated, now that he was out of jail, he could expect that at least one of the two sides would try to mess with him. He was trying to make bait out of himself, hoping to get a glimpse at how the enemy would react.

But the first group to bite were these small-time jokers. He wanted to brush them off, figuring that causing a scene in these circumstances would only prove to be a pain in the ass.

"Get lost? What? What do you mean, 'Get lost'? We're a product of bad education standards, so you gotta teach us!"

"You're the toughest guy in Ikebukuro, right, mister?"

But it seemed as though these street punks thought that the stories about Shizuo Heiwajima were more tall tale than truth, and they were simply having fun with whatever guy they found who fit the part.

"Hang on, old-timer—are you actually *scared*? You're lookin' pretty pale!" They took the fact that he wasn't attacking them as a sign that he was actually intimidated, and they stuck their faces even closer to taunt him and push him around.

If any locals who were familiar with Shizuo were present, this would be about the time they started banding together to perform a life-saving rescue mission. Everyone knew that Shizuo was the type of person who replied to a mean look with a statement like "Did you know you can kill a man with a glance? So starin' a guy down like that means you know your imminent death is a possible outcome, yeah?" before he proceeded to the destruction phase.

Some people said he had mellowed out a bit and was often seen escorting a foreign woman around, but everyone in the neighborhood knew full well that Shizuo's nature was not the kind of thing that changed overnight.

Surprisingly, however, his patience held up. Under normal circumstances, they would already be airborne at this point.

The cops might still be keepin' an eye on me. If I beat the crap outta these kids and get caught, what was the point of it all?

Thanks to the streak of patience he'd been on since last night, the length of fuse between the spark and the explosive at this moment was very, very long by Shizuo's usual standard.

The only problem was that given the possibility that Izaya Orihara was behind all of this, the volume of explosives was very, very great, indeed.

Shizuo was going to simply drive off the delinquents, but they kept inching toward the breaking point, closer and closer to the actual explosives rather than the end of the fuse.

"Why do you wear a bartender vest anyway? Huh?" one of the boys asked and lightly kicked at his outfit.

There was a sound like something cracking, but none of the boys seemed to notice. The next moment, one of the boys gathered up his boldness and shouted, "Why don't you say something, you silent bastaaaaaaaaaa...aaa...a...a........." However, his words trailed off as he flew into the sky.

Shizuo had grabbed the spokes of his bike and hurled the entire thing, rider and all, directly upward.

"...Huh?"

"Uh..."

It appeared to the other youths around Shizuo that their friend had simply vanished. Meanwhile, the ones who were watching from a distance craned their necks back to follow the action—their companion and his bicycle, tossed to a height of about five stories in the air by the man in the bartender clothes.

"Aaaaa*aaaaaaaaaaaaa*aaah!" the boy wailed. Momentum carried him away from his bike, and he flailed his limbs as he fell. But right before he would have hit the ground, Shizuo caught the boy's body with an outstretched arm. "*Gblurf!*"

The catch absorbed some of the shock, but it wasn't enough to prevent significant damage to the young man, who gurgled like a drunk passed out on the sidewalk while passersby stepped on him. His bicycle crashed to the ground nearby, its frame warping in several places.

"...So? What was that?" Shizuo asked the young toughs, a blue vein bulging on his forehead.

Perhaps the only thing that held Shizuo back from a total eruption was the youthfulness of the ruffians' appearance. But one wrong word at this point, and even a little grade-schooler with his backpack would lose his life.

The young men's instincts told them as much, and they backed away with pale faces.

"Wh-whoa, we're sorry, okay…?"

"O-oh my God, dude, I'm so sorry."

"Sorry, sir, sorry! We're just stupid kids!"

"For-forgive…*hyaaa*. Don't kill meeee!" they shrieked and scattered to the wind.

The boy Shizuo tossed into the air wobbled away, leaving his bicycle behind.

"Hey, your bike…," Shizuo called after him, but the boy froze in place briefly before running off and screaming, "You can have it! Just let me goooo!"

Within moments, all of them were gone. In the aftermath, Shizuo closed his eyes and tried some deep breathing. Close to a minute later, when the veins on his forehead had subsided, he glanced at the mangled bicycle and sighed.

"I can 'have it'…? What the hell would I do with a busted-up bike?"

In the end, Shizuo wandered around the alley with the bike over his shoulder. He couldn't just leave it in the middle of the road, and since he was someone who found abandoned bicycles irritating, his better conscience refused to allow him to leave it on the side.

He walked along, hoping to ditch it at a bike rack somewhere, but as he was far from the business area, such things were not in quick range. Eventually, he started weighing more extreme options, such as crumpling it into a ball and turning it into junk, when an odd noise became audible somewhere behind him.

"KRRRRRrrrrrrrrr……"

The "voice," which sounded like a blend of an engine revving and a horse whinnying, was familiar to Shizuo.

"…Celty?" he wondered, turning around.

Standing before him was a black horse. But there was something about this horse that was atypical, to say the least.

The curve of its long neck simply stopped without a skull on top, and the plane where it was cut was shrouded in dark shadow.

It was a headless horse.

"Huh? Ohhh…"

Where an ordinary person would run and scream, Shizuo showed no fear. If anything, he was searching for the right thing to say to the headless horse. "So, um, what's up? You're what I'm thinking of, yeah? Celty's motorcycle…kinda…"

At that, the Coiste Bodhar—nicknamed Shooter—swished its tail happily.

"What happened to Celty?" Shizuo asked with suspicion. Shooter hung its head for a moment, then arched its back and lifted its front legs.

"…You want me to get on?" Shooter swished its tail again. But after a moment, Shizuo replied, "I never rode a horse before."

Shooter froze. In just moments, shadow wreathed its entire length as it rebuilt its body into a more compact form.

Now it was not a horse standing before Shizuo but an all-black motorcycle, the familiar form of the vehicle that Celty typically rode around. Shooter gave him a cocky rev of the engine, but—

"…Sorry, I don't have a motorcycle license, either."

Shooter's engine went dead, and a cold breeze blew between the two. The creature returned to horse form, dejected enough to make Shizuo imagine it was hanging its head. But then it noticed the bicycle Shizuo cradled under his arm, and it leaned closer.

"Hmm? Oh, this? I got this from some stupid kids a moment ago…"

Suddenly, shadow tendrils stretched out from Shooter's body to grab and cling to the broken bicycle frame.

"Ohhh?" Shizuo let go of the bike, and Shooter pulled it closer to itself, integrating the structure into its shadow in a strikingly predatory fashion. Suddenly, the creature's body shrank, transforming into a shape even smaller and slimmer than the motorcycle.

It was a bit blockier than your average bicycle, but it seemed perfectly rideable to Shizuo.

"Whoa… That's pretty impressive, man," he said.

Shooter happily chimed the bicycle bell. Then the all-black device rolled over on its own and leaned against Shizuo. He glanced at it and grinned.

"Yeah, this should work. Third time's the charm."

*   *   *

Shizuo straddled Shooter and grabbed the handlebars—and with impossible acceleration for a bicycle, the mount bolted forward.

"This is just like a motorcycle or something," muttered Shizuo, who didn't need to turn the handlebars, as Shooter was turning on its own, so he held them only to keep his body propped up straight.

It could turn without losing any speed whatsoever, so if not for Shizuo's remarkable physical capabilities, he would have been thrown off already. Naturally, he couldn't understand Shooter's vocal messages. But through the fierce vibration of the mount, he could sense its panic, and given the circumstances, this led him to one conclusion.

"...So something happened to Celty?"

The bicycle's bell rang once, a convenient affirmative signal. Shizuo narrowed his eyes, feeling the summer night breeze, and squeezed the handlebars harder.

"All right. Let's hurry," he said.

Something's wrong. It's not just coincidental timing. Not when everything's piling up like this. I bet you're in on this, too, huh?

He could sense the shadow of his archnemesis lurking behind everything that was happening around him.

♂♀

Apartment building, Ikebukuro, at that moment

Izaya Orihara was in as good a mood as he ever had been.

"What's up with the frolicking?" said Mikage Sharaku.

He turned to her, beaming. "Is that what it looks like to you? Even now, I consider myself to be staying very calm."

"Calm, huh?"

Izaya had been trotting around rhythmically and humming, occasionally using shogi and chess pieces to start odd little territorial games. Most recently, he'd used his tarot deck to build a house of cards. After an hour-plus of this behavior, Mikage was thoroughly sick of him.

"You're like a child on the day before a field trip. It irritates me."

"What? You're not going to say it puts a parental smile on your face?"

"If you're supposed to be a guy who inspires smiles, then every other person on the planet might as well be Charlie Chaplin," she shot back lazily. It merely earned her a shrug from Izaya.

"My goodness," he said, "if normal people are on the level of Chaplin, then what would that make the man himself? Is there a term for someone who is even more lovable than the great king of cinematic comedy?"

Mikage clicked her tongue in irritation. From the corner of the room, Kine said, "When you tease other people for a slip of the tongue, that's when you're in a frolicking mood."

"Oh, please, Mr. Kine. If you're going to criticize me for that, it makes it that much more difficult for me to tease others in the future."

"You know that's not true...," Mikage grumbled and observed him in a fresh light.

It was clear that his mood was more *elated* than usual all day. Because Kasane Kujiragi never showed up in her hideout, they withdrew and returned to an apartment Izaya was renting. Slon, whom they suspected of being under Kujiragi's control, was still trussed up and locked in the same room as Adabashi.

But that alone did not seem to be enough material to inspire this level of frolicking. So Mikage thought she'd throw out some facts, just to see if she could hit on the real reason.

"Fewer people in here than there used to be."

Only Mikage, Izaya, Kine, and a few members of Dragon Zombie were present. That was indeed a significant drop in attendance from the original size of the group a few days ago.

Manami Mamiya had stolen Celty's head, tossed it out into public view, and vanished.

Haruna Niekawa, who was supposed to be guarding it, had not returned to base.

Slon was tied up.

Ran Izumii had suffered some kind of injury during the day and claimed he needed to recover for a while.

It was one thing to lose some members, but the lack of Haruna Niekawa's Saika power at their disposal was a big loss. And the brainwashing they'd done on the woman named Earthworm to make her accuse Shizuo Heiwajima of assault had worn off, and so she had retracted her claim.

Beyond all of that, the loss of Saika and its ability to multiply their power infinitely had to be a bad situation for Izaya—yet after receiving the news from Mikage and Kine, he remained in a good mood.

"What about this is so much fun for you?" Mikage asked. She was just going to ignore him, but he finally wore her down enough that she had to ask.

"What's so fun? Well, there are several answers...but the biggest thing is that I'm just delighted that a person I know very well vastly exceeded what I expected of them!"

"?"

"I told you about Mikado Ryuugamine, right? The boss of the Dollars."

"...Oh yeah. That name pops up a lot."

He was clearly a favorite subject of observation for Izaya, because whenever he talked about the other boy, Izaya was generally in a good mood.

"You said that everyone aside from you just sees him as a normal high school kid," Mikage said, trying to get past this to the next topic, but Izaya was obviously going to bite.

"Yes, but he only looks like a normal boy. In fact, he turned out to be far more dangerous than I expected. Since I figured that out, I've been thinking about how to bring that danger to the surface, but it turned out to be a total waste of time!"

"A waste of time?"

"Yes, exactly! *Because I didn't need to do anything to make Mikado break down in a fashion far more fascinating than anything I could have imagined!* Doesn't that just make you want to giggle and frolic? Doesn't it?"

Mikage's brow furrowed. His answer was more nauseating than anything she needed to hear right now.

"...You know, I'm not really sure how to say this, but...I feel like it would kind of be improving the world as a whole if I just killed you right now."

"Oh, I won't argue with you there. The thing is, I love people, but I don't love the world and the society we people live in. So I'm not really in favor of dying for the sake of the world, see," he said, without a trace of irony.

Kine pushed the conversation with a prompt: "So what is it you intend to do with this teenage boy?"

"*Do?* That's a cruel thing to say, Mr. Kine. It's like you're insinuating that I'm going to ruin his life somehow."

"..."

Kine merely stared at Izaya with ice in his gaze.

"...Fine, fine. I will give you a serious answer. I'm going...to let Mikado do as he will. For the first time, I think I'm going to make for a *proper observer.*"

"Observer?"

"Yes. My intent was to just stir up some trouble around the neighborhood," Izaya admitted, utterly without shame, "starting with little stuff between delinquents, then turf warfare between street gangs. Then I was going to get the yakuza and police involved...to find out how far I needed to push things to cause an undeniable reaction in the head."

"The creepy severed head?"

"Yes. It wasn't all completely baseless, as a matter of fact. But I don't suppose you'd have any interest in connections between Norse mythology and Celtic fairies, or the evidence of such, would you?"

Mikage stared up at the ceiling for a bit, then back down at Izaya. "What's...*Celtic*?"

"Exactly. That's the best you can do, so thank you for proving my point. It would be a waste of time."

"You want me to kill you?"

"Not particularly. Do you find it enjoyable to ask questions with really obvious answers?" Izaya mocked, ignoring the homicidal look on Mikage's face. He continued, "So if it's not an issue of scale, what exactly would cause the head to react? A battle to the death, with life and pride on the line? The souls of martyrs perishing in a holy war? Fighting against something nonhuman? Perhaps it could be something as innocent as babies fighting over a pacifier that sets her off."

He picked up a chess piece, turning it over in his fingers. "I considered all this infighting in the Dollars and friction with the Yellow Scarves to be part of that experiment. I tried giving anxious young men a life without security or peace of mind and threw all sorts of things into the pot: squabbles and hatreds of every stripe, warfare that transcends pure hatred, and everything in between. A real mystery stew."

He stopped twirling the chess piece over his digits and palm and suddenly threw it at the precariously balanced house of tarot cards.

"But Mikado Ryuugamine, just another one of those pieces, far eclipsed my imagination of what he could be."

The tower of paper instantly collapsed, scattering its cards all over the table.

"He's not physically strong. Compared with other boys his age, he's as frail as paper."

Izaya scooped up one of the cards that made up the tower with one hand, then tossed the little chess piece into the air with the other.

"The thing is—"

The next moment, the card he still held made a quick yet light snapping sound above the table.

"—he's kind of scary right now."

When the chess piece landed on the table again, it was split in two. Izaya waved and flapped the flimsy card in his hand.

At last, Kine spoke up again. "Do not destroy things without good reason."

"Really? That's what you're going with?"

"...Treat your pieces with respect," Kine said, his words heavy.

Izaya grimaced. "Oh, geez. I care quite a lot about both you and Mikage, I'll have you know."

"You are the kind of man who destroys everything without hesitation, even things you care about. Including that Ryuugamine boy."

"No, he's not my chess piece anymore. If anything, I'm more likely to be his, and I don't think I'd mind. He's so dangerous right now, I can't keep myself from laughing at the sight of him. And the Dollars organization is the powder magazine for Ikebukuro itself."

"Gee, I wonder whose fault that is," Mikage jeered.

Izaya spread his hands and shook his head. "It's no one's fault. A confluence of factors combined and produced that result."

"...So you're saying there's no puppet master pulling strings?" Mikage asked.

"Yes, that's right," Izaya reiterated. "No one's at fault. If I had to list a cause, I'd say a number of people around him turned out to be bad for him. Including himself."

This was Izaya's honest opinion. You might say the thing that broke Mikado Ryuugamine was his own twisted love for "the Dollars of the past," and therefore that *everyone* in his vicinity was responsible for causing this.

Masaomi Kida, who was afraid to be an open, honest friend to him.

Anri Sonohara, who tried to remain a third party.

Shizuo Heiwajima, who haplessly gave a naive boy a fascination with raw power.

The Headless Rider, who made the boundary between reality and fantasy too vague.

Aoba Kuronuma, who approached the Dollars leader to use and manipulate him.

Chikage Rokujou, who did not inflict punishment on him for creating the Dollars and thus robbed him of the chance to atone.

And Izaya Orihara, who gave him that little push on the back at the start.

Each one on their own might not have made Mikado fall to the level of sin. But the accumulation of all that weight ate away at him and pushed him down to his current depth.

Izaya considered, reflected on, and sympathized with Mikado's plight—and smiled with unbridled glee.

"But I can forgive him. I will forgive everything! They say God's love is boundless, but so is human love! No matter who else refuses to forgive Mikado for what he's done, I still will! I forgive every other person as well! They made me the audience of such a fun stage show, it's the least I can do in return!"

The way he was carrying on by himself creeped Mikage out. She sighed heavily. "Uh, all I was doing was sarcastically pointing out that you're the puppet master."

"Oh. You're not very good at sarcasm, Mikage."

"Yeah, I'm better at pounding a man's face in," she growled, starting to get up.

"Whoa, stop, stop." Izaya held out a hand to stay her. "There are some other folks you can use that aggression on for better purposes."

"Other folks?"

"The way we originally planned. I think it's time to kick out the non-human folks. This whole show is meant to make Mikado the star. It's a human drama, and the nonhumans shouldn't be messing with it."

"Does that include Haruna?"

"Oh, no. She's human. She's an incredible human, in fact; she beat the curse of the blade," Izaya declared. Mikage and Kine noticed that although his smile remained, Izaya's eyes were no longer full of mirth.

"Anri Sonohara, Kasane Kujiragi, and the Headless Rider will all need to stay quiet for a bit."

He picked up the Star, Moon, and Death cards from the table and tossed them into an ashtray that was merely a piece of interior decor and contained no butts at all.

"The problem is Shizu, I suppose. I know Mimizu withdrew her charges...but I just can't buy that he was released because he managed to get through police questioning without losing his mind."

Lastly, Izaya removed the Strength card and used a lighter from his pocket to set it on fire.

"You know how Shizu is. He's probably coming to destroy me now, and he'll destroy anything he needs to along the way. Including the entire stage I've set up just for Mikado."

Kine and Mikage knew the man he called "Shizu" quite well. Very few people who'd been living here for years were unaware of him.

The game of tag that had been Shizuo Heiwajima's and Izaya Orihara's attempts to kill each other had been one of the defining features of Ikebukuro for the past seven years.

But Kine and Mikage also knew that it was not a game of tag *like* a murder competition. It was an actual, honest competition to kill each other, and the fact that neither had died yet was something of a miracle already.

"It's one thing to do it to me. But to destroy the state this city is in... to commit *heresy* against humanity, I just cannot accept it."

He dropped the burning Strength card into the ashtray, and it promptly lit the other cards. Izaya beamed with delight at the vision. "Ah yes, I think it's time I finally take this seriously."

The next moment, the smile completely vanished from Izaya Orihara's face. The look in his eyes was enough to freeze with terror the hearts of any who witnessed it.

"It's time to make Shizuo Heiwajima go away for good."

Chat room

.

.

.

The chat room is currently empty.
The chat room is currently empty.
The chat room is currently empty.

NamieYagiri has entered the chat.

NamieYagiri: Mikado Ryuugamine, are you watching this?
NamieYagiri: If you are, log in and join the room.
NamieYagiri: If you don't, I will reveal your personal information here.
NamieYagiri: I'm very irritated right now, and not in the mood to wait.
NamieYagiri: Just get in the damn chat.

Kuru has entered the chat.
Mai has entered the chat.

Kuru: Well, well, Namie. Whatever brings you to a place like this? It is not supposed to be accessible without an electronic invitation. Did you hear about it from our foolish brother, perhaps?
Mai: I'm scared.
NamieYagiri: It's you. Bring me Ryuugamine.
Kuru: Please don't ask the impossible of us. Also, why do you interact with us so brusquely? If you are choosing to chat with your real name, would it not be more entertaining to type in your own manner of speaking? And is it really in your typical style to release real names here? Your own is one matter, but another person's identity is sacred.
Mai: It's bad manners.
NamieYagiri: Shut up.
NamieYagiri: My brother and I were given sedatives, and I'm very angry. And all of this is the fault of Mikado Ryuugamine.
NamieYagiri: I don't need any more nonsense right now.

NamieYagiri: If Izaya's watching this, you come, too.

NamieYagiri: This situation is doing Seiji no favors.

NamieYagiri: I'm going to put a finish to it all. So show yourselves.

Mai: You're scary.

Mai: Help.

Kuru: Why, it seems as though you are under considerable pressure at the moment.

NamieYagiri: Whatever. I'm going to leave this open on the screen for now.

NamieYagiri: So come right away.

NamieYagiri: Before something crazy happens to Ikebukuro.

NamieYagiri: This isn't time to be playing games with the Dollars, you little brat.

Mai: I'm scared.

.

.

.

CHAPTER EIGHT
IT TAKES A THIEF TO CATCH A THIEF

Durarara!! 12 Ryohgo Narita

Anri's apartment, night

"Um...would you like something to drink?"

"No, I'm fine," said the girl who called herself Saki Mikajima. She favored Anri Sonohara with a soft smile. "Listen, you don't need to go out of your way to make me comfortable."

Even for a single resident, Anri's apartment was fairly cramped. She was a teenage girl living on her own, but because of the circumstances of the man who'd arranged the place for her, no one gave her any trouble about it.

She almost never had visitors, nor did she ever create noise that rose to the level of a disturbance, so Anri led a quiet life, slipping under the attention of her neighbors. If anything, it was more concerning that a girl of her age barely had any friends over and hardly ever left for social outings, but nobody was interested enough to be concerned.

The only visitors her age who came over were Mikado Ryuuga-mine and Masaomi Kida, back when they actually hung out with her, and Haruna Niekawa, when she came to attack her. Now that Mika Harima spent all her time with Seiji Yagiri, Anri had no visits from any girls her own age.

Anri herself began to assume that her entire school life was going to pass without any such guests—until today, when a girl in her age range showed up.

The night was late, not the time a friend ordinarily stopped by for a visit. And in fact, the girl at the door was not a friend. She wasn't even an acquaintance; Anri had never seen her before.

She thought it was a mistake, until the other girl addressed her by name and said she had "something important to discuss about Masaomi Kida."

Anri didn't sense the kind of hostility she felt from Haruna Niekawa, so she let the girl come inside without reservation.

"Well, um…you mentioned something about Kida…"

Anri and Saki faced each other across a table. While Anri was a bit nervous, Saki looked completely at ease with being in the home of someone she had never met before this moment. An odd silence passed between the pair, so full of contrasts as they were.

"Well, I suppose I should introduce myself again. I'm Saki Mikajima. Thank you for trusting me enough to let me in on no notice like this."

"Oh, I'm…Anri Sonohara," she said, hastily bowing back in response to Saki's incline of the head.

"I know we've never met before, but we were actually in quite close physical proximity for a time."

"Huh?"

"Up until last year, I was staying at Raira General Hospital. You were there for a few days, too, after you got attacked by the street slasher, they said. Is that correct?"

"Oh…," Anri murmured, taken aback. But she couldn't recall having spotted this girl in, say, the hospital lobby. "Ummm, if I've forgotten you, I'm so sorry."

"No, no, no. We never talked in the hospital or anything like that. I just mean we were located in the same building. But it's true that I did know who you were. I just happened to learn that you were staying there at the same time—that's all."

"?"

"The thing about Kida is, he's always talking about either Mikado or you. He's shown me lots of pictures with you and him."

"...!"

So clearly, she was someone with a personal connection to Masaomi. That should have been obvious, given that she said she wanted to talk about him, but after the run-in with the two Saika wielders during the day, Anri couldn't take anything at face value.

"Um...what exactly is your connection with Kida?" she asked.

Saki considered for a moment. "How should I explain this? We were pretending to go out as far back as middle school...but recently, we became a couple for real, I suppose."

"A couple...meaning, you're, um...romantically involved?"

"I guess you could say that."

"Oh," Anri said.

It was a rather silly conversation, in a way. Because they both had personalities that were a bit off-kilter, a conversation that might normally charge the air with a prickly electricity was producing nothing more than a clammy fog.

"You don't seem surprised," Saki noted.

"Kida's always hitting on girls, so I just assumed he had many girlfriends...," Anri replied, "...but this is the first time I've actually seen one."

Saki appeared to be taken aback by this at first, but she soon chuckled. "Oh my goodness...I was so sure things were going to get very chilly in here..."

Anri turned her head in curiosity, uncertain of what she meant by this. "Why did you think that?"

"I don't know—why *did* I think that? Am I weird?"

"N-no! I didn't mean to imply that... If anyone here is weird, it's probably me..."

One after the other, their comments seemed to catch the other off guard, like the teeth of gears out of alignment. Trying to correct that, Saki said, "Actually, can I ask you something, too?"

"Y-yes. What is it...?" Anri asked timidly. Saki went right after her.

"What exactly is *your* connection with Kida?"

"Huh?"

Anri hadn't been expecting that question. Knowing the kind of typical human relationships that exist, an ordinary girl would be able to anticipate this kind of question being asked. But Anri was so far removed from "typical human relationships" that it never even occurred to her why Saki might be visiting her apartment.

"Oh, um. Well, I'm..." At last she picked up on what Saki was asking her, and she grew even more flustered. "Oh, n-no. Kida's just a friend..."

"Really? 'Just' a friend?" Saki asked, prying gently.

Anri met the look in the eyes of the smiling girl and had to turn away. Though gentle, Saki's eyes were piercing, as though they were staring right through the painting frame that separated her from the outer world and directly into her mind.

"Maybe calling him...just a friend...isn't quite right... But nothing with Kida is like..."

She still couldn't give her a straight answer. There was some measure of guilt there, of course, but more importantly, she didn't know whether it was right to tell the girl identifying herself as Masaomi's girlfriend that he had consistently asked Anri out.

"He and Ryuugamine hang out with me and help me when I'm in trouble...and..."

Even she wasn't sure how to define their relationship. Various words popped into her mind (*acquaintance*, *schoolmate*, *good friend*), but none of them seemed like the natural fit.

As she waffled, Saki leaned over until her face was close, and she said, "I've heard about Mikado Ryuugamine, too. He said the three of you hung out a lot. He said Ryuugamine couldn't take his eyes off you, either. He was always talking about how incredibly cute you are and how incredibly big your boobs are."

"P-please don't tease me," Anri said, turning away and holding her arms over her chest to evade Saki's outstretched hands.

"Ha-ha-ha, sorry, sorry. I'm half joking. But it's true that you're very pretty. I think I'm more jealous of you for that than anything to do with Masaomi," Saki said, but her smile was the same as it had been the entire time, and it was hard to tell how much she was joking about, exactly.

Her deceptive, obscuring smile never wavering, Saki asked, "Then what do you think about Ryuugamine?"

"...!"

"Is he the same as Masaomi...just a friend?" she asked innocently but with an odd kind of pressure behind it.

"Well..."

"I know we just met, so this might come off as incredibly rude, but... do you mind if I ask it anyway?"

"Um, go ahead," Anri assented.

Saki's smile grew just a bit thinner as she asked, "Sonohara...are you in love with anyone?"

"..."

"Ummm... Have you *ever* been in love?"

It was a fastball hurled square at the center of Anri's being; she held her breath with the shock of it. Saki bowed to her.

"...I'm sorry—I know it's an unpleasant question to receive. But...I really wanted to ask it."

Saki's expression was totally neutral now, and at last Anri understood. The question wasn't meant to be nasty and needling—it was simply a question that meant quite a lot to the other girl.

It seemed that giving her a vague and noncommittal reply would be rude, so Anri gave herself some time to formulate a proper answer.

It was the same thing she'd said to Haruna Niekawa half a year ago, when the girl came to kill her.

"I...don't know."

"You don't know?"

"I don't know how to love people...or what I should do to love people... I think I...I'm not capable of loving another person," Anri said, giving a rather incisive description of her own nature without including any information about Saika.

Saki didn't visually react much to that and sat listening.

"..."

"So I can't really respond to the feelings of others in kind...and I feel like I probably don't have the right to feel love or passion for anyone else. I just live off others and get various things from them—that's all."

Anri had lived her life by placing a frame between herself and the rest of the world, so that all the horrible and sad and painful things that had happened to her and continued to happen were no more a part of her than the subject of a painting. The price she paid for this was that she lived off the emotions, the happiness and delight, of the people in the painting, as if they were characters in a story she was reading.

By seeing Mikado and Masaomi having a good time, she felt fulfilled. The painting frame was just the most efficient coping mechanism she could devise to deal with the abuse her father had put her through.

Which is why I don't have the right to love others.

Anri even lived out the concept of love through Saika, so perhaps that was how she saw herself in the reflective glass of the painting frame. It was almost as if she was trying to convince herself that was the case.

Saki said, "Doesn't that feel lonely?"

Anri shook her head and put on a sad smile. "It's true that I don't interact with people much. I've been called a parasite by a classmate, and I agree with that. But it's the life I chose for myself, so I don't regret any of it."

That's a lie.

Anri was keenly aware that she had lied not just to Saki but to herself.

The conversation with Izaya during the day should have made it clear to her: She claimed she chose to live as a parasite, but it was only a means to avoid examining the dirty parts of herself.

She felt sick with self-loathing, even if it wasn't quite as bad as when she had spoken with Kujiragi and Niekawa.

"So…I don't think loneliness really factors into it at all," she explained, forcing herself to put on a satisfied smile.

"Are you happy?" Saki asked.

"I don't know. I don't even think I know what…*happiness* means to me. I just want to live quietly and not have to fight anyone…"

"Hmm…" Saki rested her arms on the table and stared directly into Anri's eyes. "You just want to live quietly and spend time with Ryuugamine and Masaomi?"

"Well…"

"You don't feel like a relationship based on dependence is lacking at all?"

"No…because even when I think hard about it, I just don't seem to understand what it means to be in love with someone," Anri continued simply. Then she hastened to add, "Oh, but…it's not like the only thing I do is leech off them—!"

Anri might view the rest of the world from a removed perspective, through her special frame, but Masaomi and Mikado were the rare people who actually reached out to her through that frame.

Like Mika Harima, who was the object of her admiration inside the painting, they had a powerful effect on her that was unrelated to feelings of love or friendship.

There were also Celty Sturluson, Erika Karisawa, Haruna Niekawa, and Kasane Kujiragi—figures who'd left their mark on her in various ways—and if anything, it was the arrival of these people that was shifting the foundations of Anri's heart.

Saki waited for the answer that Anri struggled to come up with to describe the two young men who had been the catalyst for all these encounters, and at last she said, without much confidence, "Um… Kida's not my lover…"

"He's not your lover?" Saki asked, tilting her head.

"And he's not just my friend…"

"Not just your friend?" Saki repeated, inclining her head in the opposite direction, like an insect that wasn't sure which direction to take.

"I think he's my savior."

"Savior?"

"Yes…Kida and Mikado are like saviors to me. They've given me so many things. But I haven't been able to repay it yet in any way…" Anri's eyes turned downcast and gloomy.

Saki stared at her for a few moments, then said, "You're…a good person."

"Huh?" Anri gaped. Saki gave her another smile. But unlike the one from earlier, this smile was more human.

"Well, that was…anticlimactic."

"I-I'm sorry."

"Oh! No, no, you don't have to apologize," Saki urged, waving her hand to let Anri know she wasn't being criticized. Then she sighed with relief and said, "You know…I'm glad. If you had said something like 'I'm in love with two boys at the same time and don't know what to do,' I think I would've set fire to this apartment."

She cackled to herself, despite the horrific threat in her statement. It sounded as if she was joking, but Anri couldn't help but feel that it might actually have come to pass if she'd given the other girl the wrong answer. It was *that* hard to get a glimpse past the surface of Saki's expressions.

Anri silently waited, gauging her conversation partner, so Saki continued gently, "To tell you the truth, I was actually coming here to declare war on you."

"Declare...what?"

"If you said you were in love with Masaomi, I think it would've turned into a cat fight, as they call it. I was just wondering what I would say in that situation. Should I lean into the stereotype and yell, 'Get your hands off my man, you hussy'?"

It was odd to hear Saki say "cat fight," given how peaceful her tone of voice was now. She continued, "I guess I should be happy it didn't turn out that way, though. But I can't let my guard down, because there's no guarantee you won't fall in love with Masaomi in the future."

Saki nodded at the wisdom of her own words, but Anri couldn't tell whether this bit of theatricality was honest or an act. For some reason, though, despite having never met the girl before a few minutes ago, Anri felt those words resounding within her.

"...I don't think that will happen. As I said before, I don't really know what it means to fall in love with..."

"Do you think I know it any better?"

"Huh...?"

"I'd bet it's a minority of people who actually understand that kind of thing in a rational sense. Because love and romance and all of that *aren't* rational. You don't have to know how it works—you just realize one day that you're in love. It's mysterious," Saki said leisurely, stirring up Anri's feelings.

"...But...I don't have the right to fall in..."

"Yes you do," Saki said, cutting off Anri before she could finish that dour thought. "You said you consider yourself a parasite, and maybe you're right about that...but even a parasite has the right to love someone."

"But…"

Anri hadn't considered, after she'd labeled herself a parasite, that she would be told it was okay for her to love another person anyway. She was unable to decipher what Saki was after, and Anri's eyes darted back and forth as she mumbled to herself.

But Saki was gentle with her. "I was a doll."

"A doll…?"

"Yes. Do you know…who Izaya Orihara is?"

"…!"

Why would his name come up now? What did this girl have to do with Izaya Orihara?

Saki pushed past Anri's shock and laughed. "Looks to me like you do, then. Did he do something horrible to you?"

"Well, um…kind of…"

"I see… That really sucks," Saki said sympathetically. Then she switched gears to talk about her own experience. "See, I was kind of like his doll. He told me I should fall in love with Masaomi Kida, so I did."

"…? I'm sorry—what do you mean?" It was such a bizarre, counterintuitive thing to say that it just bounced right off Anri.

But there was one thing she understood: The "shape of love" as she knew it was nothing more than the things Saika whispered to her.

The girl across from her, however, was speaking of love in a different sense than Saika's love or the love depicted in romance novels and movies—this, Anri could tell.

"Masaomi would be angry about this, but I don't even care if he hits me. I want to tell you about him. It's just… Do you want to hear? About the old Masaomi."

Anri froze. She wasn't expecting to be asked permission like this.

Masaomi Kida's past. Like Saika, it was one of the secrets they'd kept hidden from one another. She and Mikado Ryuugamine had made a promise that they would wait until all three of them were together again before they revealed their secrets.

So it was probably something she shouldn't listen to now. And she didn't like the idea of hearing about someone's carefully hidden past from a different person.

"What do you think? The thing I want to talk about might have something to do with Ryuugamine. That's why I thought I ought to tell you...but I'll let you decide if you want to hear it or not... Yeah. So let me know."

"I..."

I don't need to hear it. I trust him, Anri was going to say, but she stopped.

The tiniest note of doubt had crept into her heart.

I trust Kida?
Do I really?
Or...do I just want to look away *from the truth?*
Keep the promise.
Avoid his sensitive past.
Trust in Masaomi Kida and leave his past to him.
It would be a noble thing to do.

But at the same time, Anri wondered, *Am I really that noble of a person?*

She'd chosen life as a parasite, relying on others for everything. She had just stated as much minutes ago. She was also aware that this was nothing more than an excuse to avoid examining her own base shallowness.

But no matter her reasoning, it was a fact that she had chosen this life for herself.

It was how she had withstood Haruna Niekawa's assault and stifled Saika's attempt at a rampage.

Anri wasn't conscious of any sense of pride or beliefs, but she did know she was not going to regret her decision.

And it was this person whom the feelings down in her deepest core asked, *Why do I try to play the saint only in these situations? Am I really trying to pass myself off as human, at this late hour? A girl who doesn't know love but tries to use the love of others for her own purposes...*

Anri tried to drown out that voice, to silence it.

I live by being dependent on others. I have to be careful not to draw the ire of those I choose to leech from. I have to be careful to stay on Ryuugamine's and Kida's good sides, she told herself, but the doubts continued to rise up from the depths.

That's a lie, too. I just said it myself.

"It's not like the only thing I do is leech off them.

"They're my saviors."

"You okay?" Saki asked with concern. Anri hadn't said anything for over ten seconds.

"Y-yes…I just need…time to think," she replied and returned to her inner dialogue.

Suddenly, she recalled words someone had said to her earlier that day.

"You put distance between yourself and Mikado Ryuugamine and distance between yourself and Masaomi Kida. Didn't you?"

Izaya Orihara's words echoed inside her brain.

"You chose to stay back and wait. You had people around you who gave you affection. And you were so pleased with that, you chose to do nothing. You could have made more of a move."

Afterward, Karisawa told her that it was nonsense and she didn't need to pay attention to him. But the words were etched deep inside her now.

She wasn't able to discount what Izaya had said out of hand. She recognized where she stood.

Am I going to choose to wait again here? When that Kujiragi person told me to let go of Saika, what did I tell her?

"Plus…I have a promise to fulfill, to tell some people I care for very much about Saika. So until then, I want to remain who I was last year."

That was what I told her.

Just because she herself didn't want to change, did that mean it was the right decision to avoid looking at how Masaomi had changed, and how Mikado was changing at this very moment in time? It was a question she couldn't answer.

For one thing, she had Saika residing inside her—a fact that she had not revealed to Saki. She couldn't say for sure whether it was right for her to be involved with the two boys because of this.

When she told the Kujiragi woman, *"Maybe I'm not really human anymore. And if so, maybe I don't have the right to fall in love like a normal person and enjoy normal happiness,"* she had seemed to want to disagree with Anri.

That's right. She's...not human. I'm sure she's much further away from human than me.

But I bet she's tried to fall in love.

Like Celty.

Like Saika.

Anri had no idea that just hours ago, Celty had passionately told Shinra that nobody was more worried about Mikado than Anri. But then again, neither was she aware of the irony that Celty was now in the form of a shadow monstrosity battling against Kujiragi and her Saika.

Lastly, she thought of what Karisawa had said to her: *"I may not know all the details, but I can forgive you for everything right now. Even if you're some vengeful god of the ancient past, and you destroyed the earth once before, I still forgive you."*

She'd embraced Anri, knowing that the girl was not human. Recalling the feeling of human warmth from that moment, Anri muttered, so quietly that Saki couldn't hear her, "...I'm such a coward."

Even in the end, I relied on someone else for the final push.

After a little self-deprecating chuckle, Anri straightened out her face and said, "Please tell me about Masaomi."

"You're sure?" Saki asked. Anri nodded firmly.

"I made a promise that the time for revealing secrets would only be when all three of us are together," she said, looking into Saki's eyes, "but I don't want to use that promise as an excuse to run away anymore."

It might have seemed like a minor thing, but for Anri this was a huge decision. The world she viewed as the other side of her painting frame was now threatening to jump in, to come to her side.

"But that's not a good reason to break a promise, either...," she said, looking down briefly and giving Saki a sad little smile. "So if he's angry with you, he can scold me, too."

Saki met this declaration with silence. After a few moments, she smiled back and said happily, "You really are nice." Then, with a bit more frustration, she continued, "Masaomi might have told lots of girls that he liked them...but I bet he was serious when it came to you."

"Huh?"

"Nothing, nothing. Well, um…where do I start?"

So Saki began to speak.

She told of the past, of things Masaomi had never said to Anri and Mikado.

Of his leaner, meaner junior high days as the leader of the Yellow Scarves—and of the mistake Masaomi and Saki had made together.

♂♀

Abandoned factory, Tokyo

While Saki Mikajima told Anri Sonohara a story, there was another person speaking about Masaomi's past.

That would be Masaomi Kida himself.

"…All right. I think I get the picture."

There was only one listener.

It was the man who, together with Masaomi, had engaged in an escape sequence worthy of an action movie: Chikage Rokujou.

They were inside the abandoned factory that had previously been the hangout spot for the Yellow Scarves. More recently, it had been used by the Blue Squares affiliated with the Dollars, but after the recent attack by the Toramaru motorcycle gang from Saitama, hardly anyone bothered to visit.

While this conversation began, there was a bandage wrapped around Masaomi's clenched hand, and a cast around his entire left leg.

After they'd fled the parking garage, the truck they'd landed on had taken them in the direction of Saitama for a while, until it stopped at a red light that was quiet enough for them to get off unnoticed.

The driver was among the uninitiated, and the truck simply drove off without incident. As it went, Chikage gave it a wave with a little mutter of thanks, then took off his hat and bowed.

They caught a taxi that passed by later and rushed to a nearby ortho-pedic clinic. Fortunately, Masaomi's broken knee wasn't separated that badly, so they gave him a conservative treatment that required no surgery or hospital stay.

But it did mean his leg had to be fixed in place, which necessitated the use of a crutch. His broken right hand was also stabilized with tape and bandages.

He didn't want any trouble with the police, so Masaomi told the doctor that it was the result of beating up a postbox because he was in such a bad mood.

The doctor gave him a look of sheer annoyance, then shook his head and said, "I hear about that a lot, actually. There's some famous young man in Ikebukuro who wears a bartending vest...and now there are folks looking up to him and trying to copy what he does. When I see injuries like this, it's often a result of that copycat behavior."

The middle-aged doctor smirked and passed the time by chatting as he carried out the tests and treatment. After Chikage and Masaomi paid their bills, they hailed another taxi and took it back to Ikebukuro.

And here they were now.

Once Masaomi had called to confirm that the other Yellow Scarves had safely escaped that parking garage, he felt relief at last. Chikage observed his reaction and said, "Explain to me what's going on. We can call it even after that." Masaomi was hesitant but gave in even-tually and detailed his embarrassing past and the present situation facing him and his friend.

When it was all done, Chikage asked Masaomi to confirm that his understanding was correct. "You're sayin' the start of all this was with a gang you built back when you were just in middle school?"

"...Yeah, I guess that's accurate," Masaomi replied, biting his lip as he considered the past that had brought him here.

"And this whole hubbub going on now involves a lot of moving parts, but it's no big deal? Because it all comes down to the fact that your old buddy snapped for some reason, and you're tryin' to slap some sense into him."

"Huh? I dunno... You might be abridging a bit too much of it..."

While Masaomi was trying to show the older man the modicum of respect that the situation deserved, especially with the dramatic rescue, the fact remained that they'd been fighting not that long ago.

"So that wussy-lookin' kid turns out to be the boss of the Dollars, eh? It's a crazy world, man," Chikage said, patting the pensive Masaomi on the shoulder. "And the Blue Squares are a problem keeping you from stopping your friend. So you needed to get your gang back together to take them down first."

"...Yeah, I suppose so," Masaomi admitted, avoiding Chikage's gaze.

"Okay, I see. I see, I seeee...," the man muttered to himself.

But then he suddenly grinned.

"You dumb-ass!" He gave Masaomi a sharp head-butt.

"Wha—?!"

Masaomi faltered, holding his forehead. He was seeing stars. It was only thanks to the crutch that he stayed upright, and he glared back at Chikage through unfocused eyes. "Wh-what the hell was that for?!"

"Shut up! From the sound of it, this is all your fault for sitting around on your ass! And now I'm suffering on account of it, too... I don't deserve this kind of crap!"

"Wait—the only reason you're involved is because you stuck your own head in here!"

Chikage crossed his arms and thought for a few seconds. He nodded decisively. "Yeah, now that I think about it, that's true! Sorry about that one! My bad!"

"Were you trying to get one over on me with sheer momentum...?" Masaomi glared, rubbing his forehead.

"Listen," Chikage said, "you know you bear some fault for hitting that Horada guy, or whatever his name is, and then ghosting without another word, right? And now what? You vanished without a trace, and now you show up and say, 'I'm gonna make him stop by beating him up, if necessary'? Sounds to me like *you're* the one who could use a beating! How can you run out on a guy and then come back and act like his best friend?"

"You think I don't know all that?! Besides, if you had just gone after Mikado back when...," Masaomi started to say. "No...never mind. It's not your fault."

It wouldn't be fair for him to bring up the moment when Mikado had declared himself the leader of the Dollars—just petty. But Chikage picked up the thread he had started and continued with it.

"Yeah, if I had just accepted that he was the boss of the Dollars and kicked his ass, it might not have come to this. But I don't regret the choice I made."

"..."

"And I'm not softening on that part. If I had a time machine and went back to that moment, I'd still do the same thing. I don't know about now, but when I saw him then, he wasn't cut out to be the head of the Dollars. When the fight's already been settled, and you pretend the enemy leader is some guy you know isn't up to the task just so you can hold *someone* responsible, that's no more than blowing off steam. It ain't my style. Especially not in front of the honeys," Chikage declared, cracking his neck. "If I'm responsible for anything, then put it all on my shoulders. Just understand that the head-butt I gave you was because I was irritated at what you did. You don't use friends that way."

"...I know it's not right to get the Yellow Scarves involved in this. I'm not making excuses."

"That's not what I mean... Man, you seriously don't get it?" Chikage griped, clicking his tongue. "The friend you're using is that Mikado kid, your old buddy."

"...Mikado? Me?"

"Am I wrong?" Chikage asked. "Aren't you just thinking that if you save your buddy from trouble, it'll make up for the sin you once committed of abandoning your girlfriend?"

"I'm..."

"And that way, you can start over with your pal without feeling guilty. You don't think there's *any* element of that going on?"

"Stop it! You asked for an explanation, and I gave you one. What would you know about me?!"

" *'What would you know about me'?* "

It was as stock a phrase as they come, and Masaomi felt a clammy, lukewarm guilt rising within him. For one thing, it wasn't something you said to the guy who saved your life, and Chikage's assessment was partially correct anyway. It was because he was right that Masaomi wanted to push him away, to avoid facing the truth.

"What would I know...? Good question. Well, we've gotta figure out what's to be done next. So let's start by thinking about that."

"Huh?"

"Now, you asked me what I would know about you...and that's only what you told me now and the fact that you're pretty good in a fight..."

"Um...look... I wasn't asking for a literal answer to that question...," Masaomi hedged, feeling even more guilty now that Chikage was taking his weak attempt at deflection seriously.

But Chikage looked him straight in the face. "Now, this is the really important part. Do you *want* someone to understand you?"

"Huh?"

"It's a crucial question. It's really hard for a person to really understand another person. I've got a dozen or more girlfriends, and I could never say truthfully that I totally understand any of them. Non's pretty sharp, and she'll call me out on lots of my shit, but doesn't it frighten you to have somebody know *everything* about you, down to the deepest level?"

Masaomi felt like the conversation was drifting away from the point, but he decided to go along with it for now.

"...I'm not really good at topics like this... I thought I understood Mikado, one of my oldest friends, and it turned out I didn't know him at all..."

He could recall how, when Izaya Orihara talked about the "founder of the Dollars," he'd been unable to take the information at face value. And once Masaomi had beaten up Horada and kicked all the Blue Squares out of the Yellow Scarves, he had chosen to put distance between himself and Mikado.

Part of it was just confusion. But he was also afraid.

Afraid that Mikado Ryuugamine and Anri Sonohara would find out about his past.

Afraid that their own secrets might also be revealed.

For learning them would mean being tied closer and deeper than before. And he didn't feel he had the right to be open with Mikado and Anri, to smile and laugh with them.

So fearing that outcome, he'd taken Saki and vanished. He'd joined hands with the girl who'd wanted to know him better even after he'd betrayed her, so that he could escape the hands of his friends. He'd run away.

"I really just want…to go back to when we didn't know anything about one another, and we could just laugh and chat like normal teenagers. I want to tease Mikado and Anri and not think about anything past that."

"You know that phrases like *normal teenagers* aren't what actual teenagers use, right? That's for when you're older and you're lecturing the kids."

"…Don't tease me."

"I can't help it. From what you've said, you're just like this Mikado guy. What a pair of pals! Huh…yeah, I guess that's why you're old friends. No wonder you're alike." Chikage rested his elbows on an empty barrel and smirked.

Masaomi's brow furrowed. "Just like him…? Me and Mikado?"

"Aren't you? You and this Ryuugamine guy aren't special. You just *hate being weak*."

"Huh?"

"Damn, you really think yourself in circles, don't you? Puberty!" Chikage exclaimed. He was so bored with it all that he started checking the messages on his phone. "You're not special at all. When a little brother can't win in a fight against the bigger one, he gets desperate. So how do you get tougher than your big bro? Do you train yourself? Get smarter? Make more money to show him up? Some of them even go to extreme lengths and try to take him out in his sleep."

He beamed at Masaomi. "Whatever it is you guys are all worried about, it's no more important than *that*. Mikado Ryuugamine thinks that because he's weak, everything's gone to shit. You think that because you're weak and couldn't save your girlfriend, everything's still shit now."

"…"

"And both you and Mikado wanna do something about this weakness of yours."

"I don't…," Masaomi tried to say, but Chikage cut him off.

"If you don't have a problem being weak, then you can just leave Mikado to fend for himself."

"That's not the…"

"Not the same thing? So you think you can stop this Mikado guy, with being as weak as you are? And this guy you have *that* little respect for, you consider your very best friend?"

"...You sure like to talk, huh?" Masaomi said. It was merely a ruse to avoid answering the question, and it made Chikage grin.

"One of my honeys is a real hard-ass, and she loves debating me—it's real sweet... I guess I'd say there are a whole bunch of different mes out there, for talking to each one of my honeys. If I told you I got a nursery school license just so I could have something to talk about with one of my girls, would you believe me?"

"...And I thought I was a pickup artist. Buddy, you're the real deal."

"I'm not as clever at talkin' as my honeys, so I might not be sayin' this right...but it seems to me like you two did things the opposite. Mikado Ryuugamine chose to deny his own weakness by trying to erase everything and start over. You chose to deny your own weakness by trying to create a stronger self. That's all this comes down to."

"..."

Masaomi had no answer. He knew that if he looked for the right words for a rebuttal, they would exist. But at this moment, he couldn't find them—because he understood, to a painful extent, how it was his own weakness that had caused this situation.

Chikage decided to break the silence by changing his tone. "Hey, whatever. Let's just break it down into even simpler terms."

"I didn't think I could get it much simpler than this."

"Really? You guys are making it too complicated. Let kids be kids, and just have it out exactly the way you want it. The whole reason you couldn't just talk it over with Mikado is because you were afraid of screwing it up and wasted your time sulking about it."

"I...," Masaomi started, then hesitated.

"Make it simple," Chikage urged. "Do you want to meet up and talk with him or not? Yes or no?"

Masaomi thought he had chosen this location as a hideout on sheer unconscious instinct. But he couldn't deny that a part of him deep down had hoped Mikado might actually be here.

On the other hand, he still had hesitation and anxiety. If he did meet up with Mikado, would he actually be able to stop his friend? The incident with Izumii that evening was the source of that concern.

He had lost control of his emotions and been swept up in them, to the detriment of all else. How was he supposed to manage Mikado, then?

Now this man was telling him to follow those emotions, to do what they told him to do. Masaomi didn't know whether he was right or not. But he took a deep breath, willing himself to step forward and put it out there.

"...Of course the answer is yes! Whether I punch him or he punches me, nothing happens without meeting him first."

The latter half was just an attempt to motivate himself.

Oh, dammit. I put myself on the back foot again. It's my worst habit.

He smacked his forehead with his bandaged fist. The painkillers were still working, but the sensation from his broken fingers still rippled all the way through his body. His features sharpened, as though awakened by the pain, and his head bobbed firmly.

"Yeah, that's right. I already made up my mind. Whether it's my fault to begin with or not, no matter if Mikado cries or tries to avoid me, I'm going to save him from this situation on my own."

"Well, well. You sound a lot more selfish about it than before."

"That's right. It's all a selfish move on my part. And if he wants to kick my ass, he's free to do it all he likes afterward."

"...Ha! I like that look on your face. You're back to lookin' how you did when you agreed to fight me one-on-one," Chikage said, grinning. He smacked the top of the metal barrel with his palm. "Then that settles it! Let's go!"

"Huh? Go...where?" Masaomi suddenly had a very bad premonition. His smile froze and twitched.

Chikage gave him a very satisfied smile back. "To see this Ryuugamine guy."

"...What?"

It was all so simple, so straightforward, that Masaomi felt slightly dizzy. But Chikage seemed to be serious about it. He banged on the lid of the metal barrel with both hands in rhythm now. "Call him up and ask him where he's at. I'll even throw in the cab money."

What is he talking about?

Chikage's suggestion was so freewheeling that Masaomi's brain was having trouble rationalizing it. It took all his willpower to stay sane, keep his breathing steady, and say, "Um, he's not going to pick up a call from me..."

"Then give me his number. He should pick up if it's from a phone he doesn't recognize."

"Well, I've already changed my number since the old days...and that's not the issue anyway..."

"Yes, it is. You try everything you can think of, right?"

Masaomi had just told Chikage all about his heavy, sordid past, but the man was giving lackadaisical suggestions as if it was all fun and games to him. And for some reason, Masaomi felt that blitheness to be overwhelming.

"I'll take care of those Blue Squares kids," Chikage continued, "and you take the opportunity to go past them right to Ryuugamine."

"No...wait. This is crazy! Even you can't handle them all on your own..."

"Don't get the wrong idea. I just said I'll *take care* of them. I'm not stupid enough to try *fighting* all of them on my own," claimed the man who actually *had* destroyed a gang in Saitama single-handedly, making this a bit of unnecessary humility. "Also, I'm only helping you get face-to-face with Ryuugamine. Whatever happens after that is up to you," he said bracingly. "If you let someone else solve all your problems for you, is that gonna make you or this Mikado guy feel good about it?"

"..."

"Let's just try what we can, yeah? Our fight kinda got called off in a draw, so let's set that bet aside for now. I'll help you out from an equal standing."

This helped Masaomi remember what they'd agreed upon before they fought that evening. Chikage had suggested a bet: *"If I win, the Yellow Scarves have to work for me. But if I lose, I'll be your muscle."*

"Equal standing...? Meaning that you're just gonna do whatever you feel like?"

"Whatever the hell I feel like."

"..."

"Don't give me that look. It'll be fine!" Chikage jibed. Masaomi very nearly gave in to the sheer momentum of his cajoling but managed to hold firm.

"Either way, it's still crazy!" he argued. "If you're going to deal with the Blue Squares, you need to stop and plan out a whole..."

"...And you think I have that kind of time?"

"Huh?"

"Ryuugamine might think he's weak...but the Dollars aren't the same way," Chikage warned. He was deadly serious now, all charming breeziness gone. "I run a fairly big group in Saitama, so I know how things go...and to continue that earlier analogy about brothers fighting, there's one situation you have to watch out for."

The leader of the Toramaru motorcycle gang tapped the top of the barrel with a finger. "Even with kid brothers fighting, you don't want to attract too much attention, or the big, scary adults will get involved. And these ones aren't trying to break up the fight. They're the ones that say, 'If you help out Uncle for a bit, Uncle will make sure your big brother gets beat up.'"

"..."

"There was something about those guys you were squabbling with at the parking garage... I just got the stink of those 'scary adults' from them...," Chikage said vaguely. He then sighed with resignation and decided to speak directly.

Masaomi knew what Chikage was trying to say, and it was the last thing he wanted to hear.

"To be honest, if the yakuza get involved, even my hands are tied in how much I can help ya."

♂♀

Ruined building, second floor, Tokyo

Mikado Ryuugamine wondered where and how he'd gone wrong.

He could understand that he was heading toward the wrong result.

But no matter how often he thought about it, he couldn't understand what he'd done wrong.

Creating the Dollars as a joke with his friends, attempting to maintain his creation, using the Dollars' force for his own personal reasons—these things might be possible factors in the current state of affairs, but Mikado did not consider them to be mistakes.

But it's definitely not someone else's fault. If anyone is responsible, it's entirely me. Because I'm weak, Mikado thought, gazing dully at the ceiling.

He was in an abandoned building in an area not that close to downtown. Among other things, there had been a shoot-out here in the past, so the residents wisely chose to keep their distance from the place.

It was now the hangout spot for a faction within the Dollars—Mikado and Aoba's Blue Squares—but they used it only as a temporary home so that they could abandon it in the face of a raid of any kind.

Mikado sat on a pile of construction materials inside the building, leaning back against the wall and letting his eyes wander upward.

"What's the matter, Mr. Ryuugamine? You seem to be spacing out," said Aoba Kuronuma, who had just climbed the stairs.

Mikado sat up straight, taking his time so as not to give any hint of the anxiety he'd just been indulging, and lied, "Oh, I was just wondering about Celty's head."

He felt guilty about using Celty as a tool to hide his own weaknesses but continued on the train of thought anyway. "Why would her head just show up now, all of a sudden? It didn't seem like Izaya had any clue about it, either."

Mikado didn't know that Izaya had been in possession of the head. But he didn't know that someone had snatched it from Izaya's clutches and tossed it onto the sidewalk, either, so Mikado's assessment was actually correct on one level.

Because Celty had helped save him before, he wanted to help her retrieve her head. But even the organizational strength of the Dollars wasn't enough to get back something the police department had seized. It would be nearly impossible without having help from within the force.

At the same time, he had to wonder, "Does Celty still want her head back?"

She acted as if she was fine without it for now, but after the actual head had shown up in the center of public attention, had Celty's thoughts changed at all?

The question was one Mikado muttered to himself, but Aoba answered it anyway. "Yeah, I wonder. Celty definitely enjoys the life she has now. Maybe she feels conflicted about the head being found. She should get all her memories back with the head, right? Maybe she'll need to leave Ikebukuro after she remembers everything."

After he had revealed that he knew Celty, Aoba had heard a few stories of the past from Mikado, so he was able to offer some educated guesses of his own. "Do you feel lonely? Does it hurt to lose that urban legend you love so much, the one who was the cause for the very first meeting of the Dollars?"

"Hmm... My personal relationship with Celty has nothing to do with that anymore, so the thought of her going away really, really hurts. But if that was her own choice, then I don't have the right to stop her," Mikado explained.

But then he thought, *I wonder what the equivalent of Celty's head would be for me. I feel like I've thought about this several times before...*

Anri's and Masaomi's faces floated into his head—two people he could see right away if he made up his mind to do it.

But his own smile, when he stood next to the two of them, would no longer return. There was no way he could face them anymore. It had all come about because of his own weakness.

If curiosity killed the cat, then the Dollars, born of curiosity, had killed the ordinary life he should have led.

Almost there.

I'm almost to having everything perfect. Then Sonohara and Masaomi and I can be—

He cut himself off there.

It was only going to make his decision harder.

Mikado was staring into nothingness with no expression on his face again, so Aoba asked, "What are we going to do now?"

"First, we'll see how the Yellow Scarves act. Masaomi likes a good ambush. We ought to tread carefully."

"I see. Yes, his methods do remind me of someone else," Aoba said, his eyes wavering as he thought of Izaya Orihara.

Mikado turned to Aoba, looking serious. "Oh, right, there was one thing I was wondering..."

"What is it?"

Mikado looked into his eyes with concern. "Don't you guys have summer-vacation homework you should be doing?"

"..."

"I mean, if you're done with it already, that's fine, but I'd hate for you to run out of time to finish it up on account of me."

It was a comically out-of-place thing to say to a delinquent in a run-down, empty building. Aoba's eyes bulged briefly—but then he smiled, quite happily. "It's all right. I finished it the very first day."

From Aoba's perspective, Mikado looked like an exceedingly mundane high school student. In secret, he raved about the terror Mikado could inspire, however. Even in this situation, he *continued* to be a mundane young man.

When the man named Akabayashi showed up, he had been terrified. He had quaked in fear of a yakuza lieutenant, like any normal person would. Now he worried about his associate's school status.

He was a serious student who looked out for others. Not as an act or a persona, but because that's what he was: a normal human being. And that was the scariest thing about Mikado, according to Aoba.

He lived with over half of his being in a world that no ordinary person would ever come into contact with, and he happily, utterly accepted it as a part of normal life.

Originally, Aoba was just going to use him, but given Mikado's unique quality of having a normal, helpful side that made him frightening, Aoba began to wonder whether perhaps he could witness the sights he was hoping to see, standing shoulder to shoulder with his new associate.

Aoba, feeling equal parts anticipation and fear, wanted to see where this senior classmate of his was going to wind up. And that meant he had to make sure that no trouble got in their way.

What is Izaya Orihara plotting? Maybe he's thinking that given Mikado's current state, he doesn't need to mess with him anymore... but he's exactly the kind of sleazeball who thinks he's being an impartial observer yet can't actually sit back and observe at all.

It was a remarkably accurate assessment of Izaya, perhaps because Aoba shared some of those qualities. The man could not be overlooked, no matter the circumstances.

When the time came, he could leak information about Izaya to that Awakusu-kai fellow named Akabayashi and set up a confrontation between them and him.

Mikado watched the subtle changes in expression on Aoba's face and wondered, "Are you sure you're all right? If you haven't finished your homework, I can help you."

"Huh? Oh, no, I swear, it's all done."

It really would have been an ordinary conversation between teenagers if it hadn't been for the dilapidated setting.

Then one of Aoba's friends ruined the mood by shouting up the stairs. "Hey, Aoba! Mr. Mikado! C'mere..."

"?"

"What's the matter?"

Aoba and Mikado looked over that way and saw one of the Blue Squares rushing up the steps, worry etched into his face. "There's someone bad down there..."

"Who?" Mikado asked, but the Blue Square clamped his mouth shut and gave Aoba a meaningful look. Aoba's brow furrowed, but he sent a visual signal to answer.

"...Um, it's...a guy named *Izumii*..."

The back of Aoba's neck tightened.

Big Bro...! He actually came here?!

"...How many with him?"

"Uh, actually, I only see the one guy for the moment..."

He's alone? It wasn't Aoba's brother's usual style to do it this way. But more important than that at this point was how he was going to explain Izumii to Mikado.

Aoba was just starting to get his mind working when Mikado turned to him, nonplussed. "Izumii... You mean Ran Izumii?"

"Huh?"

"That's your brother, right?"

"...!"

Aoba was mildly shocked. "Did I...tell you about him?"

"Look, I have my own information network, you know," Mikado said, giving him a mischievous grin. "Is that a surprise?"

This reminded Aoba of something he had once said to Mikado.

"To be brief, it's because you are the founder of the Dollars. Is that a surprise? We have our own information network, you know."

He had said it when he first gave away his true nature, as a kind of threat to let Mikado realize how much he and his friends knew. And whether intentional or coincidental, Mikado had just returned the statement without any malice whatsoever.

Aoba's spine shivered. But it wasn't fear; it was fierce joy, welling up inside of him, moving him to tremble.

"...Oh, geez. How much do you know, then?"

"You were the former Blue Squares boss, right? You had a big fight with the Yellow Scarves, *caused the girl Masaomi loved to get hurt really bad, and got arrested*, right?"

"..."

"I heard you got thrown in juvenile detention or some kind of boarding school, maybe...but you were already out when you approached me, huh?"

Aoba was doing his best to keep the rising excitement from showing on his face. He even managed to affect a resigned sigh. "Well...if you know that much, there's no reason to explain any of it. If I'm being honest, my brother is crazy, and you're better off not coming into contact with him. We can go out there and head him off, but I'd recommend we change our hideout location."

"No, I'll see him."

"Huh?"

Mikado headed for the stairs, a thin smile on his lips. "He might be worried for your sake. I should probably go and explain to him what I'm doing."

"Oh? You Mikado Ryuugamine?"

When they descended to the first floor, they found a man in sunglasses surrounded by the Blue Squares, his attitude as belligerent as ever.

"Bro..."

"Yo, Aoba. I came to see ya, just like I promised, right?" he said. He had a striking burn scar across his face that drew the eye, and his very presence seemed to cast a violent menace over the surrounding area.

He was honestly the exact kind of person Mikado was least equipped to deal with, but unlike with Akabayashi the other day, he wasn't so afraid that he felt his life was in danger.

Part of it was probably because he knew this was Aoba's brother. Another factor that lessened the fear was that Izumii was clearly in less than stellar condition at the moment. Bandages were tied all over his upper half, with a light summer jacket tossed over them.

"…Um, you look like you're hurt. Are you all right?"

"Wha—? Oh. This? Sorry. Just fell down some stairs, no biggie," Izumii said, leering. Mikado bowed his head politely.

"Please take care of yourself. Anyway, I'm Mikado Ryuugamine."

"Ahhh. You're no taller than Aoba, and you're the head of the Dollars, huh? Well, I'll be damned. That's a lotta work, yeah?" he snarked, but Mikado didn't appear to be particularly upset by this. If anything, he even seemed a little bit intimidated by the menacing display across from him.

"Oh, er… Actually, the Dollars don't have a formal leader…so I'm leading the Blue Squares instead."

"Ha! The Blue Squares! So that would make you the third-generation leader, after Aoba and me. No, wait, fourth—forgot about Horada's dumb ass," Izumii chuckled. The sunglasses hid the finer emotional signals around his eyes.

What is he doing here anyway? Aoba wondered. He claimed to be here alone, but it was very possible that he had a large group of his friends lurking nearby. If it came to danger, he had to make sure that at least Mikado escaped safely.

Aoba and his companions were on edge, but Izumii just laughed once more and said, unexpectedly, "Listen…I think it's fate that we met like this. Can we talk together, alone?"

The Blue Squares bristled at this abrupt suggestion. Some man with unknown motives wanted to speak alone with Mikado? Aoba stepped in to intercept them. "Hey, Bro, you can't just come in here and mess around like this."

"Don't freak out. I'll have plenty of time to kill with you later. All right?"

"That's not the issue, and you know it." The chill between the two brothers thickened.

Mikado clapped Aoba on the shoulder, shaking his head. "It's all right. I'll talk with him."

"You will?"

"Mr. Izumii, we don't have any private rooms here, so if you don't mind, we can go upstairs instead."

"Fine with me," Izumii said with a smirk. Aoba glared at him and turned to Mikado. The Izumii before he got arrested was one thing, but there was a different air about him now, one that was much more dangerous. Letting Mikado be alone with this man was too much of a risk.

"You shouldn't do this, Mr. Mikado," he warned. "You don't know what this jerk will do…"

"It's not a good thing to say that about your own brother," Mikado lectured him, as though this were a totally ordinary situation.

Izumii laughed. "That's right, Aoba. Don't show off in front of your friends. Come and sidle up to me—'Big Bro, Big Bro'—like you always do."

Aoba ignored this mockery, intent on continuing his argument with Mikado—but the other boy smiled and cut him off.

"It's all right. I'm just going to have a chat with a former member of the group I'm leading. It's nothing out of the ordinary."

"But…"

"His Dollars membership is one thing…but I *am* technically the head of the Blue Squares, even if it's just for show. I ought to treat him with respect for paving the way."

"…"

Over Aoba's shoulder, Izumii slowly clapped his hands. "Very nice. Seems like Mikado's the one who understands proper courtesy. Isn't that right, Aoba?"

The needling tone in his voice irked Aoba, but he kept his gaze focused on Mikado. The other boy wasn't being completely careless around Izumii. If anything, he seemed just a little bit frightened. But given that he had announced they were going to talk alone, he wasn't going to hear any argument to the contrary.

Aoba glared at his brother one last time and reluctantly backed down. "All right, sir… But if anything happens, we're going up there."

* * *

"I didn't actually think you'd go along with this," Izumii said when they had reached the top of the steps. "Why aren't you more cautious? You don't look like a fighter to me. Didja think that because I'm injured, you can actually take me?"

Mikado snorted self-deprecatingly. "Oh, hardly. I can't fight at all. Even if both of your arms were broken, I bet I still couldn't beat you."

"..."

"But I don't think you would make it out unscathed, either," Mikado threatened without missing a beat. "The Blue Squares are all very good at fighting."

"So you think you're a tough guy, getting other people to do the fighting for you?"

"Oh, no. I'm very weak. Strength in numbers is my only defense," he said, his expression gloomy.

"You said me being Dollars 'is one thing' earlier. What's my status among the Dollars, then?"

Mikado turned his head to look at Izumii with seriousness written across his features. "I'm sorry to say that I don't want you among the Dollars. I'm getting help from Aoba and his friends specifically to kick people like you out of the gang."

"..."

It was such a bold and frank answer that it caught Izumii off guard. But the next moment, his sticky smile reappeared. "You got guts, man. What, you think I'm just a joke?"

"No, I don't. Just the opposite."

"What...?" Izumii grunted.

Mikado continued, "I'm...afraid of people like you. I would never treat you like a joke. I'm much too scared. But since I can't deal with you in other ways...I just want you out of the Dollars. If you had a lion in your house, and the weapons to drive it off...I don't think you'd find many people who would act like that lion is no big deal."

"..."

Izumii's expression went blank. This was not the kind of answer he'd been expecting. After a few moments, he burst into laughter.

"Ha-ha-ha-ha! Hya-ha-ha! Are you crazy, kid?! What kind of an idiot says somethin' like that?!"

He clapped his hands as he laughed. There was a note of madness somewhere deep in his voice, which set Mikado on edge. After he was finished, Izumii spotted the folding table that Aoba and his friends liked to hang around, and he sat in a matching folding chair near it.

"Okay, I see. So you're totally different from Masaomi Kida. What a little pampered Goody Two-shoes. You're funny, man. Way more interesting than Aoba, that's for sure."

Mikado's face twitched when he heard the name Masaomi. Clearly he felt something at that moment, but he did not speak it aloud. So Izumii put his elbows on the table, smiled wickedly, and got to the point.

"Mikado Ryuugamine. You said you can only rely on strength in numbers?"

"...Yes," Mikado admitted apologetically. Izumii gave him his fiercest smile yet.

"You ever think about relying on something *else*?"

♂♀

Ten minutes later

"...It's been a while. Are they still talking?" Aoba wondered, looking to the stairs with concern. He'd had his friends on the lookout, just in case Izumii knocked Mikado out and escaped from the second floor.

Whatever it was they were discussing, it wasn't likely to be your typical teatime chat. He waited, tense, until a figure appeared on the stairs. Izumii descended first, with Mikado watching him go from behind. Relieved that Mikado was fine, Aoba walked over to the stairs.

"Sorry about the trouble. That was fun," Izumii said over his shoulder to Mikado. Aoba was mildly surprised to see that he was in even better spirits than before.

"No, please, the pleasure was all mine. Thank you," said Mikado, bowing his head. Izumii gave him a little wave and headed to the exit without another word.

What's this? I've never seen my brother act this way, Aoba thought. The moment they passed each other, Izumii put his hand on his brother's shoulder.

"Mikado Ryuugamine. Fascinating kid. I like him," he whispered.

"...What did you talk about?" Aoba demanded, squinting.

Izumii ignored the question. The corners of his mouth curled upward. "The thing is, Aoba, he's too much for you to control."

"...And you're telling me *you're* up for the job?" Aoba shot back, quietly enough that Mikado wouldn't hear.

"Nah. If you can't do it, there's no way I can handle him." Izumii shook his head and whispered, "Every task's got the right tool for the job."

It was an uncharacteristically artistic turn of phrase for him.

Aoba watched his brother walk out the door, then turned back to Mikado.

He looked just the same as ever, with no sign of trouble. So Izumii hadn't done any harm to him.

But if anything, that was eerier to Aoba, and an ugly disquiet took form in his chest.

Perhaps it had been a mistake to let Mikado meet his older brother. A nasty mix of chills and frustration came over him, even more unpleasant than when he had faced Izaya Orihara.

But even then, Aoba was unable to chase down his own brother to demand answers.

♂♀

On the street, several minutes later

Once he had walked out of sight of the abandoned building, a black luxury vehicle drove past Izumii, then slowly came to a stop. The back door opened without a word, and Izumii got inside sans comment.

"Call for you."

A large man in a suit sitting in the back seat offered Izumii a cell phone. He took it and held it to his ear, waiting until the speaker emitted a deep, heavy voice that seemed to overpower anyone who heard it.

"*It's me,*" the voice said.

"A pleasure to speak with you, sir," said Izumii, quite uncharacteristically. His face was devoid of expression.

The man on the other end of the call—Aozaki from the Awakusu-kai—didn't bother with any formalities. "*Was there any movement?*"

"I got a message from Izaya Orihara. He plans to finish things with Shizuo Heiwajima."

"*I thought he was a bit smarter than that. On the other hand, I'm worried that I can't get in touch with Slon. He might be aware of what you're doing and be putting on a bluff. Give him a typical answer, then try to verify independently.*"

"What shall we do if he's really trying to kill off Shizuo?"

"*If the scumbag wants to die, let him commit suicide. Orihara might be our pawn in name, but we also owe Heiwajima for what happened with the little mistress. We maintain face by not getting involved,*" instructed Aozaki, a simple judgment cast upon the life and death of others. Then he got to the business of the day. "*What was the kid like?*"

"Just a shrimpy little squirt. Not that tall. Looks like the kind of wishy-washy guy who plucks the petals off flowers. 'She loves me; she loves me not…'"

"*I don't care what he looks like. Kids these days don't always match up between the outside and the inside,*" Aozaki growled, his voice powerful through the tiny speaker. "*Can you keep the reins on him?*"

"I'll be honest: I feel like it's too much for me."

"*I didn't expect to hear an answer like that from you,*" replied Aozaki with surprise.

Izumii grinned. "Yes, but I do like him. If he turned out to be a really snotty brat with too much spunk, I woulda crushed him and taken over the Dollars myself."

"*That's my decision to make. Don't pull any stunts on my watch. Although I'll admit, that was close to my idea anyway… I've got to say, though, it surprises me to hear that you're capable of liking anyone,*" Aozaki mocked, only to continue, "*Did you give him our present?*"

"Yes, I did."

Aozaki's voice rumbled as he threatened, *"You better not have dropped our name."*

"Even I'm not stupid enough to reveal the organization's name when I'm handing over something like *that*."

"If the cops haul that Ryuugamine kid in for anything, you and me are total strangers. Carve that into your backbone, and then maybe I won't have to snap it myself," Aozaki warned. It was a roundabout way of saying that if he mentioned anything about the Awakusu-kai to the police, he was a dead man. Although maybe it wasn't that much of a euphemism to begin with.

"...I understand," said Izumii.

"Good. Now, that thing came from a suspicious source. You're sure the kid took it anyway?" Aozaki asked.

For the first time since he got into the car, a clear, notable expression crossed Izumii's face. His mouth twisted with glee, but his tone of voice remained deferential. "He just *took it*, without fear *or* delight."

"...And he didn't think it was just a toy?"

"No, no! The kid knew what it was, and he even bowed and said 'thank you' for it. He actually started some water-cooler chat right after that, like nothing had just happened!"

"...I think I can see why a wrecking ball like you would take a shine to him," Aozaki acknowledged. When he spoke again, something in his heavy voice conjured the image of a wicked smile. *"Especially if he's that busted while putting on a normal face."*

After a few more minutes of conversation, Aozaki hung up, and Izumii handed the phone back to the man in the suit.

The man said, "You really learned how to speak. Normally, you act like a crazy son of a bitch, but around Mr. Aozaki, you're as cuddly as a pet cat."

It was quite a jab from the yakuza, who appeared to be a junior member of the group, but Izumii barely batted an eye.

"...Look, I know how to pay respects to the truly powerful. You gotta look up to the mighty, no matter what form it takes."

"Ha! You're gonna pass yourself off as that kinda guy now? You, the guy who abducts girls, gets all his cronies together, and takes cheap shots at people?"

"If that's what wins, then that equals strength."

"But you lost. Some jackass outta nowhere cracked your sternum today, didn't he?"

One of Izumii's followers must have let it slip about the fight earlier in the evening. He said flatly, "I'll crush that bastard someday, sir. He's like Kadota. I can sense the same smell coming off him."

The young mobster barked with laughter. "I noticed you're taking a pretty polite tone with me, too. So you think I'm a pretty tough guy as well?" He smiled gleefully.

The tips of Izumii's mouth curled. "Of course." The sight of the smile caused the yakuza to tense just a bit. "Violence isn't the only strength Mr. Aozaki has. It's the organizational strength of the Awakusu-kai, the financial strength, the influence he wields. And you're part of that strength, too."

"..."

"And like Mr. Aozaki, you're an individual part of the Awakusu-kai." As Izumii's dry smile grew more wicked, the other man's disappeared entirely.

"What...did you just...call me...?"

"Am I wrong? Or are you saying you're not just another pair of hands working for him?"

If the man gave a careless answer and it got back to Aozaki, he would be in big trouble. Normally in this situation, a young yakuza would crush the bridge of Izumii's nose to make it clear where they stood, but he couldn't do that now.

If he gave the wrong answer and created the impression that he wasn't a part of Aozaki's strength, this Izumii man would try to crush him without hesitation, said the sensation running through the man's spine.

After several seconds, Izumii stopped waiting for the man to answer his question. He stared forward into nothingness and spoke in a bit of a monologue.

"...To be fair, outside of Mr. Aozaki, there's only two or three guys I respect for their strength. Traugott the MMA champion, that bartender punk, and although he's softened over the years..."

Izumii trailed off. He chose not to speak aloud the name of the final man.

He knew that if he said it, Aozaki and his underling were sure to be angry.

♂♀

Pedestrian bridge

After Izumii's car drove away, the road far from the glamour of the shopping center at night was left with only muggy air and silence.

A silence that was broken by a man's soft voice.

"...Hello? There's been some movement."

Standing on a sturdy pedestrian bridge over the road was a man dressed in a fancy black suit, like a nightclub host, speaking into a phone.

"It was a vehicle Mr. Aozaki uses. Izumii just walked right into it."

The person on the other end of the call spoke for a while. When the first man spoke again, he identified his conversation partner by name.

"Right...it's just as you anticipated, Mr. Akabayashi."

♂♀

Inside a taxi, Tokyo

"Got it, got it. You can leave all of that up to me, then. You boys, ah, you can stay there and keep an eye on Ryuugamine and his friends."

In the back seat of a taxi, an Awakusu lieutenant with tinted glasses and a facial scar, Akabayashi, was giving orders to a motorcycle gang he oversaw by the name of Jan-Jaka-Jan. He ended the call and chuckled to himself.

Good grief, Aozaki. I didn't think this was the time for infighting.

But it makes me wonder what he brought and what answer Ryuuga-mine gave him.

And that makes the question, how do we react…?

At that point, the taxi driver called out, "Sir, is your eye all right?"

"Hmm?"

Only when it was pointed out did Akabayashi realize that he had removed his sunglasses and was pressing on his right eye. And only then was he consciously aware of the strange feeling around his eye: not quite itchiness, not quite pain. He'd been rubbing away at it without realizing what he was doing.

"Ah yes. Just a little tired, that's all."

"I know what you mean. My eyes have never been the same since I started getting old."

"Well, ya can't beat Father Time. I'm jealous of those young folks who can stay up all night playin' on their computers and video games," Akabayashi said. He focused his attention on the sensation in his right eye.

It almost felt as if there were a tiny whisper coming from the old scar.

I'll be damned… Feels the same as during that whole street-slashing thing six months back.

There had been a string of street attacks, which the media called "Night of the Ripper," around Ikebukuro, and he had felt a similar itch during that whole thing.

…Wonder if that sword is raising hell somewhere, he thought, referring to the cursed blade that had slashed his eye. The thought worried him. *Maybe this situation's a lot worse than I realized.*

He grimaced just a bit and got to thinking about what he should do next.

But he was unaware.

That whether from resonance between Saikas or just sheer coincidence, only a few hundred yards from his taxi, Kujiragi's Saika had transformed into an enormous net that clashed with a new, monstrous form of Celty.

And that Anri Sonohara's Saika, too, was undergoing a small change of its own.

And that at this moment, all around Ikebukuro, a great number of "grandchildren" of Saika were being born at once.

♂♀

Anri's apartment

"…"

"What's the matter?" Saki asked, alarmed that Anri had abruptly frozen while they were talking.

"Oh…no, I'm fine. I just felt a little chill…"

"Are you sick?"

"No, it's nothing. I'm fine, I think."

"Okay. I bet you were shivering with excitement, then," Saki teased gently.

Anri smiled back at her. But there was an odd uneasiness lurking behind it. She'd frozen because she'd heard an unpleasant noise in her ears, like the cursed voices of Saika going into a feedback loop.

It must have resonated with another Saika. She remembered feeling a similarly upsetting sensation when she'd caught the blow from Haruna Niekawa's Saika.

I've never felt the presence of other Saikas so strongly…

It was an omen that hadn't been there yesterday. There had been a change in Saika recently, but it had been very slow and gradual. If she was suddenly much more sensitive to the presence of another Saika, it might stem from the way she made contact with the other Saika from the Kujiragi woman during the day.

But even assuming that was true, Anri did not know why she would feel the presence so strongly now. It filled her with worry.

Did something happen to Kujiragi or Miss Niekawa…?

But she couldn't talk to Saki about all of that, so Anri was left with no one to speak to, just an uncomfortable knowledge that burdened her. But at least she could come up with a reassuring solution that would surely make things better.

I can go and ask Celty about this later.

She did not know, of course, that Celty's fate was currently intertwined with that very Saika's.

♂♀

Abandoned factory

"By the way, you mentioned an Anri a few times earlier. Would that be Anri Sonohara?" asked Chikage while Masaomi was checking on the safety of the Yellow Scarves from the old factory.

"...Huh? You know Anri?"

Masaomi was surprised because he had mentioned a "friend named Anri" in his explanations but never actually said her last name.

Chikage continued in more detail. "Cute girl with glasses?"

"Yeah."

"Tits out to here?"

"Yes! Exactly! How do you know her?!" Masaomi demanded. The mound gestures Chikage was making in front of his chest convinced him that it was absolutely the same Anri Sonohara he knew.

"She does kendo or *iaido* or some discipline like that, right?"

"...? That's the first I've ever heard of it." But as Masaomi said it, he recalled the glimpse he'd once caught of Anri holding a katana. And he knew it was most likely connected to the secret she kept from him.

"But, uh...anyway, aside from that, how do you know her?" he asked.

"Oh, I ran into her earlier today. She was with, um, what's her name, Eri. At the hospital."

"Eri?"

The name wasn't ringing a bell for Masaomi. At first he wondered whether this was some classmate of Anri's, until Chikage said her full name:

"Huh? Aren't you friends with Kadota, though? You should know a girl with black hair named Erika Karisawa, right?"

"Karisawa?! How do you know her, too?!"

"Look, a lot of stuff happened. So...that nice honor student–lookin' girl, eh? Damn, I'm jealous you get to be friends with a fine girl like her. My honeys are pretty hot, too, though. You jealous of me?" Chikage boasted briefly, but he let it drop a moment later and sobered up again. "So you aren't going to talk with Anri before you go meet Ryuugamine?"

"Well...," Masaomi murmured, "I... I think it's better if Anri doesn't know anything. Then, after Mikado and I have settled up, we can go see her together with smiles on our faces."

"If she doesn't know anything, huh…?" Chikage repeated, shrugging. He smirked at Masaomi. "You probably shouldn't take girls for granted like that."

"Huh?"

"Women are a lot stronger and smarter than us guys. Try as hard as you might to hide your cheating—they'll always see through you. It's why I don't bother to hide it in the first place."

"Wow, you're a real scumbag."

Masaomi stared at Chikage, wondering how such a man could attract so many romantic partners. Chikage ignored his gaze and continued, "Look, you're free to keep Anri out of the loop if you want. Just be careful."

"Girls these days are quite capable of inserting themselves back into the loop."

♂♀

Abandoned building

Mikado had his laptop open, sifting through various online message boards and social media sites, organizing his sources of information.

"What did you talk about with my brother?" Aoba asked.

"Oh, all kinds of stuff," he replied. "He asked me to look after you."

"No way, that can't be right. My brother would never be concerned about me…"

"I'm jealous. I'm an only child, you know. Must be nice to have brothers."

"Don't say that. I'd be better off without him."

Smiling, Mikado scolded the younger boy. "Shouldn't say that about your own brother."

"…Don't try to brush me off. I know him. I know he didn't just come here to trade pleasantries with you."

"You're right. It was a very important conversation, so I'll let you in on it. Hang on while I finish checking the boards here…"

He turned back to his screen and picked up the pace of his browsing. It should have wrapped up before too long—but in the midst of it, Mikado realized something was wrong.

"Huh...? Wh... What the...?"

He clicked on a bookmark, and a confused, suspicious look crossed his face as soon as the screen loaded.

"...What is it, Mr. Mikado?"

"What...is this...?"

It was rare for Aoba to see Mikado's face so baldly darkened like this. He looked over Mikado's shoulder at the screen.

What he saw there was a familiar chat room, filled with instances of Mikado's real name.

Chat room

.
.
.

TarouTanaka has entered the chat.

TarouTanaka: Good evening.

NamieYagiri: There you are, Mikado Ryuugamine.

TarouTanaka: My name is Tanaka. I think you have the wrong person.

TarouTanaka: What is the meaning of this?

NamieYagiri: Shut the hell up.

Kuru: The act is pointless, TarouTanaka. This person already knows everything, through Kanra's help.

Mai: It's over.

NamieYagiri: I don't care. Use the Dollars or whoever else you have to. Just find Kasane Kujiragi and Shinra Kishitani. Seitarou Yagiri is the one behind all of this, so use the Dollars to crush him, like you did to me. The Awakusu-kai, Headless Rider, Shizuo Heiwajima, and that idiot Izaya—they're all connected to you.

Kuru: It brings me no joy to say this, but I believe this chat room is finished.

Mai: So sad.

Mai: So lonely.

TarouTanaka: I don't understand what you mean. Who is Kujiragi? What are you after?

NamieYagiri: You're the one who's after something. What do you think you're doing?

NamieYagiri: Why don't you look around yourself?

NamieYagiri: I just want to bring an end to what's going on. So help me.

NamieYagiri: You have no idea about anything, and yet you're connected to everything.

NamieYagiri: Wake the hell up. You're the key.

NamieYagiri: The quickest way to end all of this is for you to understand it all.

TarouTanaka: Please stop this.

Kuru: My goodness, I'm thinking it really might be best not to interject. Perhaps this is what 100% Pure was speaking of.

Mai: I hope Aoba's okay.

TarouTanaka: Why are you bringing up Aoba?

NamieYagiri: 100% Pure is Aoba Kuronuma.

NamieYagiri: Shall I list the real names of everyone else?

TarouTanaka: Stop this! What are you trying to do?!

NamieYagiri: I'm just playing every card in my hand.

NamieYagiri: Where is that headless monster?

NamieYagiri: Same question about your girlfriend, Anri Sonohara.

NamieYagiri: You know that she's a monster, too.

NamieYagiri: You must have seen her with a katana at some point.

NamieYagiri: Want me to tell you what she did during that incident with the street slasher?

Kuru: This is quite a lot of personal information being shared. It feels like we're getting a recital from the problem-customer ledger at a particularly rowdy game arcade. But I don't have a problem with that.

Mai: Scary.

TarouTanaka: Please knock it off.

TarouTanaka: Don't ruin this place.

NamieYagiri: It's been broken for ages. Admit it.

NamieYagiri: And you broke it.

NamieYagiri: The same way you broke my research team.

TarouTanaka: Stop it.

TarouTanaka has left the chat.

NamieYagiri: Don't run away.

Kuru: But of course he did.

Mai: It's scary.

Kuru: I hate to say this, but...your ramblings are incoherent, Miss Namie. You are the archetypal "person who really shouldn't have a blog on the Internet." I never would have expected you were the type. The relationship between online and real life is such a mysterious thing.

NamieYagiri: Shut up.

NamieYagiri: Don't run away, Mikado Ryuugamine.

NamieYagiri: You once told me...

NamieYagiri: It's because it's reality that we can seek a happy ending.

NamieYagiri: You told me that hypocritical nonsense, and you ruined my life.

NamieYagiri: Don't forget that.

NamieYagiri: And don't you dare say you're not looking for a happy ending anymore.

NamieYagiri: At least take responsibility for your past words.

NamieYagiri: Are you listening?

NamieYagiri: I'm going to continue flaming this place until you show up.

NamieYagiri: Just so you know.

Kuru: ...Well, this is a very troublesome visitor we have.

Mai: Trouble, trouble.

"In an update to the years-long court case between the politician Takeru Otonobe and several major publishers and newspaper companies, a press conference was held today in which lawyers for both sides unveiled an official settlement. The case had been noted for..."

On the TV, the newscaster read from his script like always. Otherwise, Shinra's apartment was a bit draftier than before, owing to the broken glass on the balcony. The group had picked up the pieces of glass, so over half the physical evidence of destruction was now gone.

Togusa sat on the couch, watching the news, feeling the lukewarm breeze of the summer night on his skin.

The police did not show up. They didn't seem to be aware of the disturbance at the top of the building. But Togusa wasn't in the mood to relax, so he kept his phone open in one hand as he checked the reports on the TV news broadcasts.

Normally, it would be faster to check on the computer, but now that neither Celty nor Shinra were home, he didn't think it was right to use it without their permission. Yet, when Namie Yagiri woke up and learned the situation, she opened Celty's laptop at once and began typing away.

He was going to ask her what she thought she was doing, but the ferocity in Namie's manner intimidated him, so he decided to search for information from the living room instead.

"...to which Otonobe said, 'The life that I and my family lost will never return, but at least we can now look forward.' Next in the news..."

"No reports about monsters rampaging in town...," Togusa muttered, feeling relieved.

"This is a special report. We are receiving word that a police vehicle has been attacked on a street in West Ikebukuro, Toshima Ward, Tokyo."

Togusa's hand froze in the process of hitting buttons on his cell phone. "Whaaa...?"

Did Celty attack a police car in her monstrous form? Fright zipped through Togusa at first, but it turned out that the attack had been with an explosive of some kind. The police on board were unharmed, but a piece of evidence they'd been carrying had been stolen.

From browsing news sites on the phone, he could see that something had stirred the people of Ikebukuro a while ago. It was probably from people located near the police-vehicle attack who had uploaded the details en masse. Now the people who had just found out on the news were joining the conversation, producing a large volume of chaotic commentary.

What stuck out amid the noise was someone's guess: "Was it the head from earlier that got stolen?" Then came a few posts from people alleging to be witnesses, and within the span of a few minutes, it had turned into a full-on uproar with tinges of the occult: a mysterious head that seemed to be alive, stolen by a mystery attacker.

Because there had already been people wondering whether it was the Headless Rider's head, some of them began to suspect that the rider had come back to retrieve its own head.

"...What the hell is going on here?"

At some point, Yumasaki had sneaked up behind Togusa. He clenched a fist and jabbered, "Ikebukuro's finally about to become the 'demon-world city of Ikebukuro' instead! The seven days of fate are nigh! I just need to download a demon-summoning program onto my phone or game console, and then the exhilarating survival game will begin...! Gotta make it to the end!"

Togusa assumed this was all related to some anime or manga again. He left Yumasaki to his excitement and looked to Seiji Yagiri and Mika out on the veranda. They were still watching the city outside of the building, and the image without context would look like two lovers gazing out at the skyline.

Namie mostly kept her eyes on the laptop screen, but every now and then she glanced over her shoulder at the two figures on the balcony with distaste. When she looked at Mika, her eyes clouded with hatred. And when she looked at Seiji, they drowned in love.

The way her expression changed so rapidly and completely convinced Togusa that he was much better off not getting involved with Namie.

For her part, Emilia stayed calm and smiled reassuringly, but that only made Togusa worry that she was actually completely oblivious to what was going on.

Egor the Russian, who had seemed to be the most competent person there, left to go searching for Shingen Kishitani, he said.

"Does this mean the most rational person here is...me?" The two owners of the apartment were gone, so this was definitely unfamiliar territory for him. Togusa sighed. "You gotta be kidding me..."

Well, at least it sounds like Kadota's opened his eyes again. All we gotta do is smash whoever ran him over. So...where do we start, and how far do we drag him behind the van?

Even Togusa's thoughts were far from healthy. Just then, his phone automatically switched to the screen for an incoming call. The name listed was a familiar one.

Togusa hit the answer button and heard the raucous voice before he could even get the phone up to his ear.

"Hello?! Togucchan?! It's me! It's me!"

Just as the screen had threatened, it was Karisawa trying to rupture his eardrums. But something seemed strange about her. When she had called earlier, she had screamed out of joy that Kadota had woken up, but this time she was more panicked than anything.

"Whoa, what happened?! Calm down!"

"Dotachin... It's Dotachin..."

"...What *about* Kadota?!" he demanded, worry creeping into his voice. Had his condition suddenly worsened again?

"...Whassup?" asked Yumasaki, who had stopped his creepy dance in the corner of the room and was approaching Togusa now, concerned.

"I just got a call from Dotachin's father," Karisawa said. She paused, and then her voice grew even louder through the phone speaker. *"He*

said Dotachin left a letter and vanished from the hospital...even though they said he couldn't walk!

"*What should we do?! I'm sure Dotachin went to get even with the guy who ran him over!*"

♂♀

Ikebukuro

Somewhat earlier in the day...

Black and white flashes and blurs contrasted wildly from street to street.

Above them, golden hair rose and shone, bright against the dark of night.

A bicycle colored a perfect black seemed to absorb all light that hit it, and riding atop it was a man wearing a bartender's vest—Shizuo Heiwajima.

He clung to Shooter the shadow bicycle with sheer arm strength alone, withstanding a bucking, rodeo-like series of jolts and abnormal positions. The vehicle was in bicycle form for the first time ever, and it didn't seem to be getting the hang of the idea; it hurtled along in a violent and awkward manner.

But at this point, they were working in perfect harmony, as if one single creature. With each ferocious push of the pedals, Shizuo caused black shadow to spill from Shooter's gears, filling in the fine cracks and holes in the road to keep them moving smoothly.

Shooter raced through the night city, turning left and right, and occasionally even grabbing the sides of buildings with its shadow to run along their surface.

After about ten minutes of riding, Shizuo heard an odd sound like metal scraping.

"...Huh?"

Shooter's shadow rustled more fiercely than usual when the sound happened.

"What's that sound?"

He wanted to keep pushing onward, but the sight of something troublesome in the street ahead caused Shizuo to stop pushing the pedals. "Hang on. Come to a stop."

Once he could tell that Shooter was slowing down, Shizuo looked to the other end of the street again. There was a roadwork sign ahead, and there were cones at the entrance to a narrow alley. Standing before them was a group of men in work uniforms.

But there was something wrong with them.

They weren't getting to work at all. They were just standing at the entrance of the work zone.

"That seems weird."

The metal scraping sound was definitely coming from down that side street. Yet, there didn't seem to be any construction work happening.

Shizuo reacted to the abnormal scene by tapping Shooter's handlebars with a finger. "Let's just go around the back way."

Shooter rang its bell in a rhythmic whinny and took off through the darkness.

They made their way around the other side of the district, appearing only to the untrained eye to leave the work zone behind. But at every other road that led into the same area, they saw the same signs and groups of stationary workers.

It was a district of office buildings, and after work hours, the people completely cleared out. He saw a few luxury cars along the curb that looked out of place, but since nobody was inside, he let his attention move past them.

"...You want to go on ahead, yeah? If so, ring the bell once for me," Shizuo said when they were within sight of the street. Shooter's bell rang a single time; Shizuo inhaled and exhaled briefly and rolled his head to crack his neck.

"Guess that's that, then. We gotta climb the side of a building," he announced, a preposterous solution—if not for the fact that Shizuo on his own could probably climb the side of one of these structures. And so could Shooter, who was able to ride along the wall to an extent now. Even without his actual owner and rider, Celty, the vehicle could probably manage to get up, with a little help.

Shizuo began glancing around the buildings in the vicinity, looking for one that was unlikely to attract attention. Just then, one of the men in the work outfits noticed Shizuo. A moment later, *all* of them were looking straight at him.

"Oh, shit."

Shizuo considered going somewhere else to avoid scrutiny, but he came to a stop when he saw the workers' eyes.

At first he thought it was the effect of the warning lights next to the roadwork sign, but even the parts lit by the nearby streetlights were obviously abnormal.

The whites of every last worker's eyes were *red*.

Shizuo had seen those eyes many times: in the park on the evening known as the Night of the Ripper, and just a few hours ago, inside the police station where he was briefly held.

"Okay...I get it. So *these* guys did something to Celty," he said, putting it together. A few seconds later, he told the horse, "Too bad. Celty's my good friend."

Deep down in his voice, there was a core of rage, hot like liquid magma. Shooter shrank away from it—and so did the road workers who were approaching now.

"C'mon... Don't hold back... Let's blast straight through 'em!" Shizuo put his weight into the pedals of the bicycle, then thrust with his feet as if he were trying to kick the very earth with the bicycle.

Shooter channeled Shizuo's anger, letting all that energy course into the ground.

Instantly, like a fighter jet being catapulted off the deck of an aircraft carrier, Shizuo and Shooter shot forward toward the little alley.

They did not turn back to see the poor men under Saika's control floating through the air unconscious like so many sheets of paper.

♂♀

Back alley

In the center of a street complex sealed off at all ends, there was a tiny intersection among a series of buildings, where a number of alleys overlapped.

There was no traffic light; one of the alleys was barely wide enough for a motorcycle to ride down. The other road had space for a small car to fit, but it was off-limits to cars in the first place. It was the kind of route that only those who knew the area well would take, on foot or on bicycle.

It was a quiet place to begin with, sparsely visited, and a number of the buildings nearby were currently under construction or renovation. One of them had a construction crane attached.

All of this was why Kujiragi chose this place for her hunting ground.

And thanks to those she had controlled with Saika, she was able to close off the entire area along the bigger roads under the guise of "construction." If the police noticed the abnormality and investigated, the ruse would be up very easily, but thanks to her Saika within the police force, she was able to get it officially acknowledged as a night road-work site.

That meant the intersection here in this block was out of direct view from the surrounding areas, a little space entirely segregated from the rest of the city around it.

But of course, all you had to do was look into the sky over the intersection to believe you were in some alternate dimension isolated from the rest of the world entirely. It was certainly the case for Seitarou Yagiri, who stood in the alley and gazed upward.

"My goodness…"

There was ample, varied emotion in his voice, and he could offer no further comment. Instead, he turned to Kujiragi, cold sweat shining on his cheeks.

"Just to be clear, this is the Headless Rider…the dullahan's body?"

"That is correct. The shadow has gone berserk without a rational mind governing it, but when it calms down, it should return to a fleshy body just like a human's again."

"I see… This is quite a change," Seitarou said, looking upward again.

Normally, dark night sky would be visible between the buildings. But at the moment, there was an eerie, totally black cloud that seemed to be stretched between the structures. It was almost as if a black aircraft of some kind had crashed and gotten stuck between them.

Saika, in silver wire form, was tangled around the black shadow in endless ribbons, the tiny metal ropes creaking and screeching eerily as they ground against the shadowy thing.

"So you have total control over Saika, eh? And you can just…let it go from your body like that?"

"My control will work for a while, even after it has detached from my hand. But if I go too far away, it will likely revert to its katana form."

"And I'm supposed to just pick that thing up and take it home?"

"If you have the means to contain the body once it has been freed from its current constraints, be my guest," Kujiragi said flatly. It wasn't sarcasm, just a statement of fact.

Seitarou held up a flashlight without a word. He saw spears of shadow occasionally escaping through the wire mesh and scrabbling at the sides of the buildings. He winced and said, "I'll pass. The kick that Shingen's goon gave me still aches."

"A wise choice," Kujiragi replied before turning to the subject of her plans. "A courier is bringing the head this way now."

"Oh?"

"I believe that if the head is returned to the captive body, it will regain its rational mind. If I then use Saika to again sever the head and body, it should be possible to take the body."

"…And will the body actually sit still if that happens?" Seitarou wondered skeptically.

"To a dullahan, the head is its memory storage," Kujiragi explained. "When the memories of the past return, it should automatically revert to its original personality."

"And in that case, what will happen to its memories in Ikebukuro, as the Headless Rider?"

"I do not know that. There is little precedent for this."

Seitarou found it odd that she said there was *little* precedent, rather than *none at all*, but he decided it was better not to inquire further. "I see… Well, if the memories are erased, it will make the process of training and brainwashing simpler," he said without emotion.

Kujiragi's eyes traveled downward. "If her memories were to vanish, that would make me happier," she mumbled, to Seitarou's surprise.

"Why do you feel that way, too? Because if she escapes from my watch, you will not have to worry about her vengeance?" he asked, as if it was pointless to worry about.

But Kujiragi just said, honestly and without expression, "*Because it suits me better to have a romantic rival's memory wiped.*"

"???"

This was very curious to Seitarou, but he didn't have the chance to ask about it, because—

"Mr. P-President!"

—an employee he'd left behind along the alleyway rushed up, out of breath.

The men he'd brought with him here today were old companions who were aware of the shady side of the business—people from before Yagiri Pharmaceuticals got bought out by Nebula.

In other words, they were stout fellows who knew what they could handle. And yet, the look on this man's face was practically of sheer terror.

"What is it? Is the head here?" Seitarou asked. It didn't seem likely that he would be this afraid of a severed head, and he couldn't imagine that Kujiragi's hired courier would be stupid enough to just walk around holding the head in the open.

So he tried to calm the employee down, assuming it was something else—but even this wasn't enough to stop the man from trembling in terror.

"There's some weird guy, Mr. President... He just started rushing down the road at us, and...!"

It was then that Seitarou, his employee, and Kujiragi all heard the whinny.

A whinny that was strangely cute. Almost like a bicycle bell.

"Lrrrrrrrrrrrrrrrrrrrrrrrrr————"

"Is that...?"

The Coiste Bodhar? Did it follow its owner?

Kujiragi immediately looked upward. The massive black shadow was still writhing up there, but the movement was noticeably duller, less crazed.

Is it regaining its reason? she worried, but there was no other sign of change yet.

"..."

She couldn't risk any trouble, though. The Coiste Bodhar, like the head, was one of the major aspects that made the dullahan what it was.

It didn't seem capable of doing anything on its own, but she had to be cautious.

Should she return a part of the wire-form Saika to her palm? She considered it for less than a second before putting a stop to the idea—one of Seitarou's men, holding a stun rod, shot around the corner of the alley ahead and slammed into the side of a building. He lost consciousness and slid to the ground.

"Huh...?" Seitarou gaped, too stunned to react more capably than that.

"Eeeep! I-it's coming!" one of his men screamed and took off running past Seitarou and Kujiragi.

"Hey! Wait! *What's* coming?!" Seitarou demanded, but the man kept going down the other side of the alley and vanished around the corner. "Worthless buffoon," he swore and turned to examine his fallen employee, a cold sweat now running down his back.

What in the world was it around the corner that had shot him like a human cannonball? Despite the huge, freakish *thing* hanging just above them now, it was the unknown intruder that filled Seitarou with boundless fear.

And in the next moment, *it* came into view:

A man in a bartending outfit riding a bicycle, slowly turning down the alley.

"...Guh?" He gawked.

So much for a company president being able to maintain his own dignity. He simply couldn't put two and two together. "Hey, Kujiragi... what is that?"

Kujiragi didn't miss a beat or bat an eye. "Which are you referring to? The bicycle? Or the man seated upon it?"

"Both, obviously!"

"...The bicycle is, I suspect, the Coiste Bodhar. The rider is Shizuo Heiwajima."

"?"

Seitarou was confused. An individual's name wasn't what he'd expected to hear. So Kujiragi elaborated as succinctly as she possibly could.

"*He is the human being with the least human attributes*, as far as I am aware."

*　　*　　*

Shizuo squinted ahead, slowly pedaling on Shooter. He could see a middle-aged man holding a flashlight and a woman with glasses who resembled a secretary.

"…Hey. Are you people with those clowns who tried to attack me?" Shizuo demanded, temples slightly pulsing. Then Shooter moved of its own accord, pulling back into a little wheelie. "Whoa, whoa, what's up…?"

And then Shizuo saw it.

The huge black *something* trussed up between the buildings over the narrow little alley intersection. It was hard to tell, but it was definitely darker than the night sky and the urban illumination reflecting off the ground, like a black hole swallowing all light.

He couldn't tell what was going on at first, but when he saw the occasional spear of shadow emerging from the mass, Shizuo recognized a similarity to something he was quite familiar with.

"Is that…Celty?" he muttered. Shooter rang the bell once in affirmation. "Hey…! Celty! Can you hear me?!" he called out, with no response.

Shizuo clenched his teeth and turned to the middle-aged man. "What the hell did you do to her?"

He got off Shooter and put his hands on the walls of the narrow alleyway, blocking the other man's path. The man took a step back, properly intimidated.

However, the secretary-like woman stepped forward and replied, "I will answer that."

"…What?"

"Yes, what is above our heads now is what you once called Celty Sturluson. But at this moment, it is nothing but a monster without reason and rationale."

"…"

The woman spoke in an utterly matter-of-fact way, despite the feral-tiger menace that Shizuo posed. She was neither helpful nor malicious but simply stated the facts mechanically.

"What are you people after?"

"She… Pardon me, what used to be 'she,' is now nothing more than a product for a transaction," the woman revealed, to her companion's shock.

"Um, Kujiragi—?"

"There is no point in hiding the facts," the woman named Kujiragi stated crisply before turning back to Shizuo. "She is not a human, nor a pet, nor an endangered animal. She is just a freak. I am engaging in the business of hunting her and selling her to a wealthy buyer—that is all. You have no good reason to interfere."

Scrunch.

Something crumbled. The sound came from the vicinity of Shizuo's right hand, which rested against the building wall.

In fact, his fist was about half-buried in the concrete surface. He had simply grasped it with the power of his fingers, like squeezing through wet tofu.

"…"

The middle-aged man froze, but Kujiragi did not react in any way. He seemed to find her lack of reaction reassuring, as he said, "She's right. We're not engaging in some wicked crime. It's just business. It doesn't violate any law. After all, there's no legal recognition of monsters, is there? All I want to do is pay money for something that should not exist in the first place. I would appreciate if you stayed out of this."

Shizuo clenched his teeth and sucked in a deep breath.

"…I see your argument. You seem to have your reasons," he said, surprisingly calm by his standards. He looked at them and then up at Celty. "I don't complain when the motorcycle cops chase Celty around. She bears fault for what she does. It all makes sense. And maybe you folks have a reason that makes as much sense as the cops riding those bikes."

"Thank you for understanding."

"But—" Shizuo took a step forward. That was all it took to immediately compress the atmosphere into something more oppressive. "—I don't give a shit about what the law says. Celty's a very good friend of mine."

The middle-aged man felt as though a lion that had been sitting calmly inside a small cage with him had suddenly stood up. Anger even infused Shizuo's breathing. He walked slowly forward as he talked.

"And now you're going…to treat her like a thing…to sell her off…" He leaped forward into a run with all the velocity of a cannonball. "And you expect me…to stand there and *watch*?!"

Rubber smoked on the surface of the asphalt where it had been rubbed off the soles of his shoes. The businessman was helpless in the face of this superhuman advance. He couldn't move fast enough to avoid Shizuo's oncoming arm, which was more like some heavy industrial machine arm than mere bear or tiger fangs as it closed in on his throat.

But when he was just inches away, the distance between the two men suddenly grew.

"Gblerk!"

Kujiragi grabbed the man's collar and hurled him violently backward. He flew about ten yards and landed flat on his back. In other words, she had thrown a full-grown man, one-handed, at a speed faster than Shizuo was charging. While she wasn't as powerful as Shizuo, it was still baffling strength for a thin woman like her.

"K-Kujiragi, why did you...?" The man gurgled, feeling as if a roller coaster had just deposited him onto the ground.

Without turning back to look, Kujiragi told the man, "Please keep your distance."

Her attention returned to the obstacle before her: Shizuo Heiwajima.

The moment she faced him, the Saika binding the shadow cloud overhead began to rustle. The wire-form blade screeched exuberantly, scraping against its own length.

"...I did not want to draw your presence here."

To Saika, Shizuo Heiwajima was just another target of her affections, but an extremely desirable one. The various "children" of Haruna Niekawa's Saika had been terrified of Shizuo ever since the Night of the Ripper—but Anri's and Kujiragi's Saikas considered him to be a very special human.

Wary of her precision control over Saika going awry, Kujiragi had tried to use a "child" within the police department to hold Shizuo off, but it seemed as though there had been trouble with Izaya Orihara that had caused that to go awry.

"What? Whaddaya mean?" Shizuo demanded, frowning.

Kujiragi stood in his path, her face flat. "I am only speaking to myself." She gave a little wave of her head and stared Shizuo right in the eyes. "You said that Celty is your friend."

"Yeah, so what?"

"Can you still call Celty Sturluson a friend in that state?"

Is Celty a friend or not?

With that simple question, Kujiragi raised her eyes to the sky. Shizuo followed her gaze to glance at the wriggling thing up there—indeed, it wasn't a human or any other existing animal.

It created endless little spears of shadow through openings in the wires, ceaselessly scrabbling against the walls of the nearby buildings. It was a pure monster, one that exuded no higher intelligence beyond instinct.

That was Celty now.

But Shizuo wasted no time in saying, "Of course I can. What's the problem?"

He gave her a look like *Why would you even ask that question?*

Kujiragi's eyes widened just the tiniest bit. She asked, "How can you say that a monster that has abandoned its intelligence and human form is a friend?"

"Is this really the situation for a question like that?" he shot back. It was hard to tell whether Kujiragi really meant him harm, and he found he was rapidly losing a target for his anger. "Listen, all this stuff about monsters? I've been called that and worse since I was a kid. I've snapped and lost sight of everything around me and given Celty headaches on more than one or two occasions."

He squeezed the wall he was holding as he thought about his past experiences. The concrete crumbled through his fingers into mere dust. "But even then, she would hear me out afterward. She didn't write me off."

He looked up and repeated, "She would hear me out."

His eyes left Kujiragi to find an emergency stairwell on a building just ahead. It was fixed to the outside of the second floor, the kind that had a ladder that could be lowered to the ground in case of emergency. "So now it's my turn to hear *her* out."

Shizuo headed past Kujiragi toward the emergency stairs. He didn't know what was going on with Celty now, but he might as well start by breaking those wires holding her in place.

Suddenly, Kujiragi's hand was around his wrist.

"Hey, stop it. I'm not one to hit a..."

He stopped partway when it occurred to him. The slender woman was *holding him back* with a strength that was unthinkable given her size.

And yet, he couldn't see her expression from here.

"...I feel...jealous."

Shizuo detected the tiniest bit of emotion in her voice, something that had not existed before this point.

"Of you…and of Celty Sturluson."

It might have been jealousy, as she said, but it sounded more like mourning.

"I never had anyone to hear me out."

While her strength defied her appearance, it was far from Shizuo's. He could brush her off if he wanted, but Shizuo wasn't sure whether he should.

Then he heard Shooter's bell ringing over his shoulder. As if it were trying to rush him along.

"Oh…sorry, I'll go help Celty now," he said briefly, realizing that Celty should be his priority at the moment, and tried to work himself free. "Look, I don't care about your problems…but if you want, I can listen to 'em later."

He put his other hand on her shoulder to pry her grip off.

"Requesting cease of activity," said a familiar voice behind his back.

Shizuo stopped yet again and turned around slowly.

It was indeed a familiar woman standing there. She was holding up a gun with a silencer as if out of some movie, in the kind of pose that those movie stars assumed.

She wasn't like Horada, who had once shot him. This was the stance of a professional.

Shizuo sighed and said, "Vorona…"

The woman whose name he called felt her mouth dry, and she glared at him.

"I desire for you to be pacified, with absence of resistance…Sir Shizuo."

♂♀

Alleyway

Neither Seitarou nor Kujiragi knew that Shizuo and his new steed, Shooter, were not the only ones who had broken through the blockade around the alleyway.

When Seitarou's employee ran down the other end of the path, he noticed that the men in roadwork outfits under Saika's control were no longer there. But he wasn't going to be bothered with a detail like that. He needed to get away and call for help as soon as possible.

As he ran, he took out his phone so that he could get in touch with the others in Seitarou's stable—until a jolt hit his jaw like an electric current, and he blacked out.

As she dragged the man into a trash-collection area in the alleyway, Mikage Sharaku thought, *Not only was he no sweat, he didn't even notice I was there. What an amateur. And those slaves of Saika were no big deal, either.*

There were a number of men in work uniforms there, just as unconscious as Seitarou's henchman. They'd all taken fierce blows to the jaw or temple, and they wouldn't recover for quite some time.

I was hoping I'd come across someone with at least a little backbone.

She thought of the people at Rakuei Gym, the business her family owned. Even beyond the circle of her own relatives, the tougher members of the dojo were not easy to conquer, even for Mikage. There was one young man, named Kisa, who was attracting attention for the speed at which he picked up techniques.

I haven't sparred with that big lug yet, though...

He was a promising newcomer who boasted the greatest height in the dojo, but she just wasn't that interested.

It's more fun to fight against the guys who really wanna kill you, Mikage reflected. She sighed and tossed Seitarou's follower into the trash.

"I gotta say," she murmured, looking up at the crane hanging over the construction site, "he really does love his heights..."

♂♀

Construction site, upper area

Perched on the edge of the building frame, next to the construction crane, was Izaya Orihara.

The beams were still exposed at this unfinished stage. Around the platform was a heavy vinyl curtain meant to keep the work tools, materials, and people from falling off the side. Izaya stood where there was no scaffolding or vinyl for protection, surveying the area below.

One good gust of wind could have pushed him off the edge, but Izaya happily stood as far out as he could go to watch the proceedings below.

"I guess this was the right building. That's a good sign."

Even a building under construction would, of course, have security guards. But said guards were currently unconscious.

A few of the Dragon Zombie motorcycle gang's members stood behind Izaya, but Kine was not one of them. He had said "being an accessory to murder isn't my job" and left earlier.

"That sounds just like Mr. Kine. He pretends that his old self never existed," Izaya muttered, watching the area at the foot of the building. "It's like they're setting it all up for me. All the annoying monsters gathered up in one place."

It would be perfect if Anri Sonohara were there, too...but I suppose that would be too much to ask.

When he'd gotten word of the abnormal roadwork going on, he'd had the Dragon Zombies check it out and learned that the workers were likely under Saika's control. Assuming that something was going on, he took those followers of his and sent them into a building under construction. The results he got back were greater than he had ever imagined.

That enormous black mass stuck between the buildings had to be Celty. He didn't know what had happened, but it seemed clear that it was the work of Kasane Kujiragi, who was down on the ground below. The president of Yagiri Pharmaceuticals appeared as well, giving him an idea as to the connections at play.

If Yagiri Pharmaceuticals takes control of the Headless Rider's body, that removes one element of uncertainty. Then I just have to figure out how to eliminate Kasane Kujiragi.

For the last few minutes, he'd been calculating his plans to this end—until the sight of the man who showed up after Seitarou completely obliterated those thoughts.

Shizuo Heiwajima.

His absolute archrival, the man he'd just sworn to eliminate for good. Why was he here? Izaya could only wonder at the sequence of events that had brought him there, but such questions were ultimately useless.

Izaya Orihara thanked humanity, rather than God. Through whatever means, fate had brought Shizuo Heiwajima there at this moment.

But Izaya's pure joy that welled up in his breast at the incredible coincidence turned into irritation and hatred upon recognizing Shizuo.

He considered, once again, that he and Shizuo Heiwajima were never meant to mix. Just the knowledge that he was living somewhere in the world was enough to spoil the innocent joy within Izaya.

Why did he hate that man so much?

Perhaps this question came to him out of a premonition that it would likely be the last time he ever needed to ask it.

What a funny thing. I think that no matter how we met, I would always have wanted to kill Shizuo Heiwajima.

He had once been told—he forgot by whom—that his hatred of Shizuo might have stemmed from some kind of complex. Did he despise Shizuo because he felt the other man had something he lacked?

That was probably part of it. But that was only *one* reason, and he knew it wasn't enough to explain the entire magnificent structure of his hatred.

A variety of reasons came to mind. He had dozens—perhaps even hundreds—all of which were true, but none of which felt like more than just a small part of the puzzle.

In the end, there was really just one reason that he hated Shizuo. It was likely something he shared with the other man. And the fact that they had even this *one* thing in common made him sick to his stomach.

The reason was simple.

He just really pisses me off.

*   *   *

All of it, the grudge and the hatred, began with that very first impression.

And so Izaya had to accept that he really could kill a person for a reason that simple.

He let his eyes close, then opened them slowly.

It was the same little smile Izaya always wore.

With his everyday expression on again, he thanked coincidence for bringing him to this moment and looked to the foot of the building once more.

Shizuo and Kujiragi were grabbing each other, and someone had a gun trained on them both.

I guess that must be Vorona.

With the creaking of monstrous Celty and the wires around her as background material, an enraptured Izaya murmured, "Ahhh...this is a very good position..."

"If they just separate a bit more...I might not have to use the crane..."

♂♀

Alleyway

They had no idea they were being watched from above.

And if Shizuo looked up, his attention would be drawn to Celty anyway.

Not that he had the wherewithal to look upward at the moment.

"What are you holding there, Vorona...? That's not a toy, is it?" Shizuo asked her.

"This is not a demonstration," she said. "I am sincerely holding this firearm."

She was wearing a very eye-catching riding suit. A large messenger bag was on the ground a short distance behind her. It hadn't been there before, so she must have brought it with her.

"What are you doing here?"

"I am in the midst of a different manner of commerce than the duties I perform with you. It is impossible to shut my eyes to violence against my client."

"Listen, we don't have a rule against doing side jobs, but *at least* be smart about what you pick, yeah?" Shizuo drawled.

"…Your reason for being composed is indecipherable. Do you have some matter with which to question me?" she lobbed back.

Shizuo considered what to do. In the corner of his vision, he could see Shooter's shadow wavering with seeming indecision.

Recognizing the situation, Kujiragi let go carefully, so as not to agitate Shizuo. Her face was as emotionless as before. He still wasn't quite able to decipher exactly what kind of expression she'd been making earlier—but now wasn't the time for that.

Shizuo lowered his hands and said, "Question you? Well, I dunno if she's your client or what, but you're pointing the gun to protect this chick, right? I let go, so you can put that away now."

"…"

Vorona looked as if she was going to lower the gun but was undecided about something. "There is a matter of which I must apprise you, Sir Shizuo."

"What is it?"

"Within the first fortnight of May, inside a schooling facility of Toshima Ward, you should have experienced being stabbed with a Spetsnaz knife by a woman wearing a helmet."

"Oh yeah. That happened." He sighed deeply. "That was you, right?"

"…"

"Look, I'm not an idiot. It was obvious from the riding suit," he said, which was perfectly true. But he seemed to feel bad about saying it. "Plus, even beyond that…I just kinda had a suspicion about it…"

"I cannot consent to the answer that you were cognizant. It is a house built on sand. If you testify that you are aware of all of creation, then why did you not shatter my vertebrae with your strength?!"

Even in these moments of psychological vulnerability, Vorona's verbiage was nearly baffling. The more serious she felt about something, the more extreme her use of the Japanese language became. It seemed she felt that the more overwrought and obscure the choice of words, the more polite it was. But to everyone else, it just made her harder to understand.

"...I'm used to the way you talk by now," Shizuo remarked. "And I'm not gonna do anything to someone I worked with long enough to get used to."

"It differs from your personality. It is indecipherable," Vorona protested, lowering her gun just a bit.

"Look...what makes me snap is when things ain't *right*," he said, eyeing the gun. "If you've got a proper reason for shooting me that's fair, then shoot me or stab me or what have you; I won't get mad. The only exception is if some guy I've never seen before shoots me. Whether he's got a good reason or not, that'll piss me off."

In fact, Shizuo did have a wide range of fury. When Seiji Yagiri stabbed him with a pen and gave a preposterous answer as to why, he had thrown the young man quite hard. But once he understood that those actions were done out of honest love, he let him off with a restrained head-butt. When Chikage Rokujou challenged him to a direct fight, the emotion he used as fuel was something other than anger.

The downside of this was that when faced with something unfair or dishonest, he would flip out over even the smallest of slights; it was his biggest flaw.

"..."

Vorona silently looked on.

"C'mon, Vorona. What is it you actually want to *do*? Just tell me that first," he said, an honest question addressed to the first junior work associate he'd ever known. "I'm your senior, so the least you can do is look to me for help, yeah?"

What...?

Her heart began to waver at this question. Or perhaps it had already been unsteady, and this was just the first time she actually noticed it.

What am I...doing? I want to destroy Sir Shizuo. To understand and confirm the strength of humanity.

It was a desire she'd always held about those who were considered powerful, going back to her days in Russia. It was one of Vorona's purest desires, as twisted as it was.

But now that she had experienced ordinary life here with Shizuo and Tom, there was another emotion budding within her, beyond the simple urge for destruction.

No... I am...not allowed to have an ordinary life. Why did I choose to betray Father and President Lingerin...?

She shook off her moment of weakness and tried to view Shizuo as an enemy again. But even then, she couldn't keep her heart steady.

No, not like this. Sir Shizuo and I must crush each other with everything on the line...or all of this is meaningless... It cannot happen in this way, as a kind of afterthought...

Vorona was shocked to realize her mind was finding excuse after excuse not to shoot Shizuo at this moment. Now there was no way she could argue against Slon's assessment that she had grown tepid and soft.

What...?

What do I want to do?

Flying by the seat of his pants, Seitarou suddenly yelled at Vorona, "H-hey! What are you doing? Shoot him dead right now!"

"...Hey, old man." Shizuo's voice caused all the air around them to freeze. "That don't sound like it's exactly *right*, now does it...?"

There was a clear note of irritation in his statement. He turned around slowly and met Seitarou's gaze. The look caused the other man to tremble. It froze Seitarou in place, causing the muscles in his hips and back to dislocate slightly, paralyzing him with pain.

"...!"

"When you kill a person...you gotta be prepared for them to kill you first... So if you're gonna order Vorona to kill me, that means you're tellin' her to accept dyin' in retaliation, right? So you're sayin'...you want my precious coworker to perform a job that you know might kill her...? Is that it?"

"W-wait! I... I'm...!"

Seitarou tried to scrabble backward, hands and feet flailing, like an insect. The man who had barely batted an eye at the various freakish things he'd seen today now felt his heart leaping into his throat with terror at the slowly approaching man in the bartender's vest.

The distance between them closed without mercy before Seitarou could so much as regret his decision.

"..."

Vorona hadn't recovered from her confusion in any way. She tried to point the gun at Shizuo as he closed in on Seitarou. But Kujiragi placed a hand over her arm and motioned her to lower the weapon.

"You were not hired personally by President Yagiri. You do not have an obligation to obey his orders."

"..."

"Both you and I are being misled by personal feelings. My rule from experience is that bringing personal sentiments into work will lead to bad results. It should be reflected upon and learned from."

In Kujiragi's head was the image of Ruri Hijiribe, whom she had once treated as a transactional product.

If only she hadn't let personal sentiment move her. Or perhaps if she *had* let it motivate her to save the girl, it might have resulted in a different outcome. She shook her head—it was pointless to wonder now.

"Let us pull back now, to sever this vicious cycle."

"Wh-what?! Kujiragi! What are you doing?! You have to save me!"

Seitarou couldn't hear the women's voices, but he could tell from their actions that something bad was happening.

Kujiragi then cruelly informed him in a businesslike manner, "My duties for the day do not include your personal protection, President Yagiri."

"Wha...?"

She held out her palm to indicate the large bag Vorona had brought, and she gave him a deep, formal bow. "As we agreed, I have brought you one of the products. I shall deliver to you the dullahan body and Saika at a later date."

"W-wait! Isn't *that* the dullahan's body? That thing atop the buildings?! What are you thinking?"

"That it will be difficult to recover it at this moment."

If they used the contents of Vorona's bag, it should be possible to get it from its current state back to the original humanoid form. But she wasn't anywhere near confident that she could keep a newly cognizant dullahan trapped with Saika *and* deal with Shizuo Heiwajima. And with the way the cursed sword was aflutter at Shizuo's presence, she wasn't sure it would even be successful at keeping the dullahan trapped for long.

So she concluded, with that robotic flatness of affect, a most human of rationales.

"I do value my life, after all."

As she listened to Kujiragi speak and Seitarou wail, Vorona lowered her gun.

I can't. No matter what I do in this situation, I cannot fulfill my desire. To destroy Sir Shizuo will require...more resolution than I am able to summon at this moment.

This side job was, in fact, intended to give her that resolution, but she wasn't prepared to run across Shizuo right in the middle of it like this. Like Kujiragi had said, it was probably best to withdraw now.

Vorona steadied her breathing, trying to control herself, and looked up at the night sky. She saw the shadow mass again and squinted.

But at the same time, she noticed something wrong. It was something she noticed only because her past work history had required her to be very observant of details.

Do they engage in construction at such a late hour in Japan?

The black creature was tangled up in wires just about in the center of the space between buildings.

But above it, near the top of the building currently under construction, there were bright lights shining. Not the red warning lights for the benefit of airplanes, but something brighter, like halogen lamps.

If this was true, then the workers up there could easily witness what was going on below. Curious, she moved a few steps to get a better view of the top of the building.

The results were still suspicious. She could see a forklift perched right near the edge of the structure. It had to be very close to the edge indeed if she could see it from the street. She squinted, finding that rather dangerous, and noticed something else.

The payload end of the forklift was actually extending over the edge—and it was loaded up with building materials of some kind.

Right next to it, there was a small human figure...

...!

And then Vorona realized *what it was the person on the roof was about to do.*

"Sir Shizuo!"

She was running before she knew it—right for Shizuo, who was still approaching Seitarou Yagiri with laser focus.

Just scant seconds later, she slammed hard into Shizuo's back.

"?!"

He lost his balance and stumbled several steps forward. "Hey, what the hell was that for, Vor—?" he shouted, turning back to protest.

And he witnessed a cavalcade of steel beams and rebar crashing down onto the spot where he'd stood just seconds before.

"Wh… Wh-wha…?"

Seitarou was now well and truly stunned at what was happening around him. He couldn't be blamed for his abject terror, given that he, too, had just been in that spot moments before. If he hadn't been backing away, he would be dead right now.

One of the bars bounced and landed right next to him, but Seitarou was unable to budge even the tiniest bit.

Kujiragi's eyes were bulging; she had no idea what had just happened. Apparently, this was not part of her plans.

But at this point, Seitarou didn't care anymore; he just cursed fate and prayed that the employee of his who ran away would come back with reinforcements to save him—the employee who, unbeknownst to him, was currently unconscious in a trash-pickup area.

Shizuo was just as immobile as the rest of them.

He was so unable to process what had just happened that he even forgot to breathe. All he could see was an endless pile of steel beams sprayed around a tiny, cramped alley.

And before him, trapped under one of the beams—Vorona.

"…Vorona!"

He snapped out of it, racing to her side and hauling the beam off her with one hand.

Her body was still visibly intact, so it hadn't been a direct hit straight off the drop. But the metal materials had clearly struck her on the bounce, as her suit was ripped in several places, the skin beneath bloodied here and there.

"Hey, are you all right? Vorona! Hey!"

"…Sir…Shizuo."

"Oh, good! You're alive! You'll be okay!"

"Worry is...unnecessary. I had an evasive calculation, but I was unable to avoid the jumping building materials."

Her speech was much more understandable than usual, which was probably a good sign. It was hard to tell whether the force of the steel beams was affected by the bounce off the pavement or whether it was just thanks to her excellent physical fitness, but she didn't seem to be in mortal danger.

"You idiot... Don't risk your life for my sake..."

Indeed, Shizuo might have taken the hit directly and lived. But in the moment, Vorona had feared for his life and pushed him out of the path of the debris. Now Shizuo was full of regret and shame that she had been injured in his place.

He wanted to say something to her—but the situation would not allow him to.

"Sir Shizuo!"

Vorona, lying flat on her back, gaped at what she witnessed. Shizuo put two and two together and looked upward.

What he saw was quite abnormal, indeed.

Falling from the roof of the office building under construction was *the entire forklift.*

First it tilted like a seesaw, until the entire body began to flip over—and it fell right toward them, like a scene in a movie.

Time flowed very slowly for Shizuo as it happened before his eyes.

Just before the forklift fell.

Standing to its side.

Looking down at them.

A man, his face unclear.

Just for an instant—even the color of his clothes was warped by the halogen lights.

But with a foreboding that was close to certainty, Shizuo spoke the name that came to his mind.

"...Izaya?"

And then the forklift was plummeting toward Shizuo and Vorona.

Seitarou wailed, and Shizuo secretly hoped it would simply flatten him. It never even occurred to Shizuo that any of the debris might strike and kill him in the process.

But no one could believe what happened next.

Shizuo leaped to his feet and rushed at the falling forklift to give it an extremely simple and powerful shoulder tackle.

In sumo terms, this would be known as a *buchikamashi*, a violent shoulder strike.

Shizuo, of course, had no experience in actual combat disciplines. He was just following an instinct that told him to give the falling object a body blow. But the impact of such a blow at zero range would be devastating.

The vending machines Shizuo typically threw weighed around six hundred pounds. Depending on the contents, they might get up over a thousand.

But the forklift falling down on them easily cleared a ton. And it was falling from the top of the building—even if it wasn't the final height of the finished project.

It was a weight that spelled certain death—but Shizuo literally knocked it away. The moment he made contact, the forklift's trajectory changed dramatically, accompanied by a tremendous crash as the vehicle bounced off at an angle and slammed into the partially built structure, breaking through the concrete wall and tumbling inside it.

Following the racket of the wall's destruction, silence reigned over the alley. No one was in any position to speak.

Unavoidable death for any other human being had been no match for the pure physical strength and hardy body of Shizuo Heiwajima.

Even Vorona, whose life had just been saved by this, was unable to believe what had just transpired.

She'd seen Shizuo kick cars like soccer balls. She knew that knives couldn't stab through his skin.

But she had never been cognizant that he was allowed to be *this* ridiculous. Would bullets even pass through his body? She was in the presence of a superhero out of an American comic book. Vorona's definition of *human* was crumbling before her eyes.

"...You okay?" Shizuo asked, breaking the silence he had created.

He smiled with relief when he saw that Vorona wasn't freshly injured. "Yeah, you seem okay to me."

Then he tilted his neck to crack it and turned his back to her, rotating his left shoulder. "Sorry...Vorona."

"...?"

"I'm about to do somethin' that ain't right. I can't complain if you shoot or stab me for this one." Then he turned toward Shooter, which was farther down the alley, and bowed. "And you... You looked to me for help outta this situation... I'm sorry. When Celty's back to normal, you can kick me all you want."

If you judged him on words alone, he might seem even calmer than usual.

But everyone in his physical presence could tell—even Seitarou, who didn't know Shizuo at all—that something else was behind his words.

Anger.

Pure, simple, endless emotion.

Shizuo was a fiery mentality compressed to its most potent state, walking in human form.

The words he'd just emitted to Vorona and Shooter were probably the last impurities of other emotions before he burned them all away.

Vorona, Seitarou, and even Kujiragi could all imagine what would happen once he had finished expelling everything that held him back— and they felt an itch from deep in their bowels that urged them to *run*.

When Shizuo had seen Vorona outside the police station, he'd felt the greatest rage he'd ever felt well up inside him. But within hours of that, he'd been acting normally. After that, he'd tossed a teen into the air and had a talk with Shooter, which even Shizuo had thought was a sign that his anger had fully subsided.

But he'd been wrong.

He'd thought that pushing his emotions underneath the surface meant his anger had calmed. But all it meant was that the actual *thing* lurking at the pit of his emotional center had not allowed that anger to be expressed.

He instinctually knew that this tremendous rage, fiery enough to evaporate boiling magma, could be reserved for only one man.

And there he was.

Having just maliciously injured Shizuo's coworker Vorona.

Shizuo strode forward, directly into the construction site, through the hole the forklift had blasted in the building's wall.

As he did so, Vorona noticed that Shizuo's right arm was dangling limp from the shoulder and seemingly immobile.

"...Sir Shizuo."

But she couldn't stop him.

It felt as if stopping him now would be akin to defiling something sacred. Perhaps it was some cheap illusive form of religion in her heart, born of her admiration for human strength.

In any case, there was no one present who could stop Shizuo now.

♂♀

Shizuo entered the building and began to slowly climb the stairs.

His phone received an incoming call signal. Without taking his eyes off the stairs ahead, Shizuo accepted the call and put the phone to his ear.

"Hey, Shizu."

It was the voice of the man who had just tried to kill him—and Vorona.

"So that didn't kill you, huh? You really are quite a spectacular monster. But the concept of you protecting a human being is nothing short of farcical."

"..."

"Maybe I brought this up before. Do you think saving people is going to make them like you? Oh, but maybe you feel something special for that Vorona girl, perhaps? I had you pegged for the pedo type, the way you were looking at the Awakusu-kai mistress. But I guess a literal monster being a figurative monster is just a bridge too far, eh?"

"..."

"By the way, are you sure you ought to be abandoning Celty? Do I need to point out what an absolutely evil person that Kujiragi woman you let escape is?" he mocked, both insult and warning in one, as he so often did.

Shizuo said nothing. He just kept climbing the stairs. Only when he was about halfway up the building did he finally speak.

"Izaya." His voice was calm, betraying not a shred of anger.

"...*What is it?*" Izaya replied.

Shizuo's voice was still calm.

"...*So long.*"

It was the last remaining shred of Shizuo's sense of reason.

"..."

Once Izaya had confirmed that there would be no follow-up, he gave his own parting words before hanging up.

"*Yeah, good-bye.*"

His voice, too, was calmer than it had ever been before.

One wouldn't suspect that they were about to engage in a brutal fight to the death.

♂♀

A bit later, Vorona and Kujiragi ventured into the building.

"Do you really intend to follow him?"

"...I deliberated the necessity to see it through. Stopping me is meaningless."

"You might suffer directly."

"Your assistance is not required," said Vorona, who wobbled toward the stairs despite the wounds all over her body.

Kujiragi, who was unharmed, just shook her head. "I suspect that attack was the work of Izaya Orihara. He is the savior who gave me my freedom but is also a clear and dangerous enemy. I will need to ascertain the outcome."

"..." Vorona continued in silence.

Kujiragi followed behind her. Inside this building, she could still maintain her link to Saika. If Izaya and Shizuo were to take each other out, she could then collect the dullahan's body and safely perform the final transaction.

But while this calculation was for the benefit of her business, the truth was that she also wanted to see the conclusion of Shizuo and Izaya's clash.

Surprised that she had this looky-loo sentiment within herself, Kuji-ragi walked steadily behind Vorona. But right when they were about to reach the stairs, a voice stopped them.

"All right, ladies, that's far enough."

They turned back to see a young woman. She looked like a fighter of some kind, based on the toughness and litheness of her physique.

"Sorry. But Izaya told me not to let anyone else inside," she said with a shrug.

"When we announce a refusal, what is the state of the outcome?" Verona asked.

"...You must be Slon's partner, huh?"

"!"

Vorona's eyes widened at the mention of her partner's name.

"And you must know about Slon, too," the woman said to Kujiragi, but she gave no reaction, either affirmative or negative.

Mikage Sharaku twisted and waved her body left and right.

"It's no fun fighting against someone injured...but if you really insist, I can play with you for a while," she said, sounding bored about it. She glanced at the ceiling. "What's happening up there is probably the world's stupidest and most meaningless fight to the death."

She shook out her limbs and put on a rare smile.

"But for whatever reason, I just don't feel like letting anyone inter-rupt it."

♂♀

Alleyway

"Th-the head... Must at least recover the head," Seitarou muttered to him-self, writhing along the ground like an insect. He made his way through the mess of steel beams and rebar, fighting against the pain in his back.

But just when he was one pace away from reaching the bag Vorona had left on the ground in the alley, a pale shadow swooped in out of nowhere and snatched it up.

"!"

When Seitarou looked up, he was aghast.

Standing there in a white gas mask was the Nebula scientist Shingen Kishitani.

"Shingen…!"

"Fwa-ha-ha-ha, look at you now, Seitarou. It reminds me of when you would beg me on hands and knees as students."

"Shut your lying mouth! I never begged you for anything! Why are you here?!"

"Hmph. I thought it would be a good opportunity to falsify some old tales of school, but it seems to have failed right out of the gate," Shingen said, his shoulders drooping theatrically. He took a few steps away from Seitarou and made a show of opening the bag. "I've been watching this all from the shadows. I have to say, that Shizuo really is something. I nearly unleashed my bladder when he struck that forklift. Did your drawers stay as dry as mine, I wonder?"

"Answer my question!"

"I heard that Miss Kasane had kidnapped my son. I figured that following you would lead me to the right place, and sure enough…"

"Your son…? What do you mean?" wondered Seitarou, who knew nothing about Shinra's abduction. When Shingen pulled the head out of the bag, Seitarou's voice went ragged. "Oh! Ohhh…what a sight for sore eyes… Such beauty! That belongs to me! Give it here!"

"But of course. I am a gentleman. When I find something that belongs to someone else, I turn it in to the police…or to the owner directly."

Owner. The choice of words caused the breath to catch in Seitarou's throat.

"You… You don't mean…"

"Well, how fortunate that the owner happens to be so close by! A sure sign of my own good virtue!" Shingen exclaimed. He looked up—at where the cloud of shadow was still held prisoner by Saika's wire cage.

"W-wait, Shingen! Your son is the one I'm thinking of, right? He's in love with the dullahan's body, yes?!"

"I will not deny it. Oh, my son and his troublesome interests. How can he consort with a woman who won't even call me Papa or Father?" Shingen joked.

"Wait!" Seitarou shouted. "Don't give her back the head! According to Kujiragi, it might completely erase all of her memory of life in Ikebukuro!"

He wasn't worried for Shinra's sake, of course. It was just more likely that if the dullahan was restored to normal, Shingen would snatch away everything he'd been working toward—and his warning was an attempt to prevent that.

Shingen just laughed and shrugged. "I suppose that is quite possible. As a researcher for Nebula, if I were on the clock, my first priority would have to be bringing back the head...but while on vacation, I cannot help but want to run an experiment to see if putting the head back on the body will really erase its memories or not!"

"You would ruin your own son's life?!"

"Oh, he'll be fine. Shinra's a tough kid. If Celty loses all her memories, he'll just start the whole twenty years over again!"

"You... You knave!" Seitarou roared.

Shingen ignored him and grandiosely announced, "Life is an endless process of trial and error! Ha-ha-ha-ha-ha! And away we go!"

With that, he hurled the head straight upward.

It went only a few dozen feet and bounced harmlessly off the wall of the second floor.

"..."
"..."

The beautiful woman's head hit the ground and rolled.

In the embarrassing silence that followed, Shingen crossed his arms and proudly declared, "It is said that the human head weighs between six and eighteen pounds. Celty's head was on the lighter side; I'd wager closer to nine. Can *you* hurl a nine-pound dumbbell up to the top of a building? I certainly cannot!"

Seitarou stared at him, aghast, but Shingen merely hid behind his white gas mask and excuses. "What did I just tell you? Life is a process of trial and error."

And then a man appeared from behind Shingen and scooped up the head. "Are you certain you're using that phrase correctly?"

Shingen glanced at him and pointed forcefully to the sky. "Aha! The experiment resumes! Your turn now, Egor!"

Egor smirked uncomfortably at the obnoxiousness of Shingen's command but proceeded to take off his jacket to use it as a sort of primitive sling into which he placed the head. The next moment, he rotated rapidly and hurled the head high into the air.

"Nooooooo! That belongs to meeeeee!" Seitarou cried, the sound echoing off the walls of the alley like a movie effect.

The head shot upward like a cannonball until it reached the shadow cloud trapped inside the wires.

And Shooter, which had been watching this unfold in bicycle form, instantly transformed into a horse.

♂♀

Building under construction, first floor

"..."

The women inside the building faced off in silent tension, until Kujiragi suddenly looked up into the corner—in the direction of her wire-form Saika.

"What's up?" wondered Mikage, without losing any of her battle preparedness. Kujiragi did not answer immediately.

Eventually, she sighed without adjusting her features and said, "I suppose it's true... Shizuo really is the wild card."

"?" "?"

Mikage and Vorona merely glanced at her, punctuation marks over their heads. She elaborated sadly, "The final transaction was a failure.

"With Saika distracted, I was unable to keep *her* under control."

♂♀

Building under construction, top floor

Izaya Orihara sat on the lip of the building, watching the scene unfolding below as he waited for the arrival of his archenemy.

He'd already evacuated the Dragon Zombies from the rooftop. He knew that the average motorcycle-gang member would do little more than briefly delay Shizuo Heiwajima. He might pass them on the way up and beat them to a pulp, but that wasn't Izaya's concern.

There was one odd thing happening under his duly watchful eye. Saika's wires snapped and broke, falling down to the center of the alley intersection below.

Then the huge mass of shadow contracted all at once and took the form of a human figure. The figure cast out little shadow tendrils like a spiderweb to stand upon, making it look as if it was floating in place.

But that part was not particularly surprising to Izaya.

At first, he believed that Celty had regained her intelligence—but something was wrong.

The figure that emerged from this transformation was not in a motorcycle riding suit, but in heavy, medieval armor. It wasn't reflecting the light, so it had to be made of that same shadow material.

And this time, most uncharacteristic of all, Celty carried a human woman's head under her arm.

He recognized the head, of course.

The shadow-born thing looked smoothly all around and detected Izaya's presence. It then created a set of shadow stairs, still cradling the head, and began to walk toward Izaya.

Once it was within earshot, Izaya called out, "Hi there, Celty. How does it feel to have your head back?"

But there was no response.

After a short pause, the head under the figure's arm slowly opened its mouth. The voice that emerged spoke to him in an eerie tenor that seemed to register in his eardrums and his mind at the same time.

"[Who are you?]"

It was a statement that would cause certain people to despair upon hearing it.

"Oh, I see. So you're not the Celty I know any longer."

Izaya smiled thinly to himself. But he did not ask the questions about the human soul and the afterlife that he'd been so eager to learn. Instead, he pushed her away.

"But the thing is, I don't have time to mess with the likes of you right now anyway."

"[...]"

"If you don't know who I am, get lost."

The head was silent for a time, until it spoke again in the same manner. *"[Forget that you saw me, human.]"*

He watched the dullahan descend toward the foot of the building and exhaled a deep breath. Then Izaya looked up to the sky and chuckled to himself, "Oh, it's just so laughable. There has to be a limit to stupidity."

There was no one around to ask the meaning of this statement, just the expansive darkness of night.

However, at that moment, he was aware that the shining stars that had been overhead just moments ago had vanished. The sky was entirely black, without even the reflection of the neon lights of Tokyo. As if a giant lid had just been placed over the sky.

But even that, in this moment, meant nothing to him.

Izaya Orihara waited and waited.

For this moment when he would close the book on the grudge that had been abandoned for long years.

Grudge? That gives him too much credit. Does one call the instinct to smash a hateful cockroach a grudge?

He considered his "grudge" with Shizuo Heiwajima beneath the starless sky.

Shizuo would be coming to kill him very soon. He had attempted that any number of times before, of course, but this time was clearly different. What he had heard from Shizuo's voice over the phone had not been annoyance or irritated anger, but pure, undiluted *murder*.

Sure, Izaya might have dropped a little forklift off a building, but he hadn't been trying to kill Shizuo. He just didn't mind if the guy died as a result.

And yet, Shizuo was coming to kill him. Perhaps if Vorona hadn't gotten hurt, Shizuo wouldn't feel such bloodlust at the moment, but if that was the case, it seemed laughable that he was ready to murder for the sake of a human being.

At the same time, Izaya felt annoyed. He couldn't accept that this preposterous monster should be able to use his boundless violence to extinguish the fates of human lives.

There was a parade happening around Mikado Ryuugamine, a procession that drew many others into its gravity.

Izaya Orihara found himself surprisingly excited about the whole thing, thinking he might catch a glimpse of a side of human nature he had never seen before.

He loved all of humanity's actions. He wasn't going to complain about the outcome of the festival, no matter what it ended up being. If Mikado had an abrupt change of heart and made up with Masaomi Kida without any more trouble, Izaya would respect that conclusion.

Because that would be the life Mikado Ryuugamine chose.

Life.

To live as a human.

That was all Izaya really wanted from others, at the root of it all.

When he made himself a pest, interfering in the way of life that others chose, it was just because he wanted to see their human reactions. If it resulted in their downfall or even the end of their lives, well, seeing the end points of their human lives would also be entertaining to him.

But monsters could overturn the fate of a human being. With their magical powers or supernatural strength.

And Izaya couldn't have that.

Humans had to determine the outcome of human lives.

The forces of nature were unavoidable, but it wouldn't be right if a being with the strength of a full typhoon were to have a human personality, act like a human, and manipulate human lives.

Izaya briefly recalled something a friend had said in the past.

"If Shizuo's a monster, what does that make you? You've got differences in strength and intelligence, but you can hold your own against him, so how do you view yourself? Do you want to be the hero who defeats the monster? Or do you treat this as a territorial squabble between monsters, where you're staking your claim to those humans?"

Izaya wondered why he would have remembered such a quote at this moment, but he was grinning before he realized what he was doing.

"You've got it all wrong, Shinra," he murmured to no one in the dark. "I never held my own against him."

Within his narrowed eyes there was a kind of resolution that hadn't been there before.

"What I'm about to do now is a good old-fashioned monster hunt," Izaya said, using the excuse that he had arrived at after considering dozens. "Maybe if I beat him, I'll finally feel like I'm a human being."

The word *grudge* also included the insinuation of mudslinging.

Ah yes. I suppose other people might think what I'm saying isn't entirely fair. At this point, Izaya realized he was actually feeling rather refreshed. *I'm going to erase Shizuo Heiwajima from the earth over mere dirty accusations and slander.*

Was the fact that he felt better knowing this actually just a sign that he was incredibly human already? If so, he didn't care.

As long as Shizuo Heiwajima vanished, he would be free of this shackle.

Did Izaya like humans because he was a human being himself? Or did he enjoy observing their foibles from on high, like some god? Izaya was fine with either case being the answer, but there was one thing he didn't like.

Shizuo Heiwajima was a monster who transcended the limits of humanity. By eliminating Shizuo, Izaya might be able to see himself as a human being. All the exaggerations he had ever made might become truths.

When Namie or Shinra got snarky with him, he might be able to sincerely reply, "Of course I love myself. I am a human being, after all." It felt strange, but he even considered it worth risking his life for the sake of that one stupid phrase.

He stood there on the silent, empty roof, wearing a vaguely human smile, thinking of the world that existed beyond his release from this accursed relationship—and came to a conclusion that would hold true, no matter what that world was.

"Yeah…I love humanity."

The words melted into the starless black sky, like his last will and testament.

INTERMEDIATE CHAPTER
PROUD, DOOMED RESISTANCE

Durarara!! 12 Ryohgo Narita

Shinra's apartment

"Man, this ain't funny, Kadota!"

"Let's hurry. At this rate, Kadota's death flag is going to get triggered."

"I have no idea what that means, but you better not mention the word *death* again, dammit!"

Togusa and Yumasaki were rushing to leave the apartment and look for Kadota after getting the update from Karisawa on the phone. When they were at the entryway, the intercom buzzer went off.

"Dammit, not now!"

It was probably Shingen Kishitani or Egor. Emilia was still here, so they could open the door and switch places with the visitor, Togusa decided. He promptly turned the handle—and in the next moment, opened his eyes wider than they'd ever been in his life.

Even Yumasaki's eyes, which were famously tiny, were agape such that the white could be seen entirely around his irises.

"...Yo," said the grinning visitor, sweat damp on his face. "I thought I was coming to Kishitani's house... What are you guys doing here?"

"Ka... K-K-Ka— Ka..."

Togusa's blood pressure rose at the suddenness of it all, and he found himself unable to speak properly. Instead, it was Yumasaki who shouted a greeting to their unannounced visitor.

"K...Kadota! You're all right?!"

"...So that's what happened, huh?" Kadota said, sitting on the sofa, after his full update from Togusa and Yumasaki. Emilia had examined him and prescribed him a painkiller cocktail. He had at least changed from his hospital gown to the set of his own clothes that had been left in his hospital room, but his father hadn't brought the signature beanie with them, so he seemed different from usual.

With all of that out of the way, Togusa asked, "But why are you here?"

"...Oh, I just figured I'd be able to get some pretty strong drugs here. My hunch was dead-on."

"Stay in the hospital, man! Why did you slip out in the first place?!"

It was a perfectly reasonable question, and Kadota looked guilty answering it. "Well...I'll admit, I did the hospital wrong. I'll go back to apologize properly later."

"I wasn't asking for you to show off! I'm saying they weren't sure if you'd even be able to walk properly or not!" Togusa pointed out.

Even Yumasaki joined in with a rare rebuke of Kadota. "That's right! Me and Karisawa are one thing, but what would Azusa think if she heard that?! I know you're aware of how she feels about you! You've got a 3-D route open to you, and you're just going to break that flag?!"

"...Sorry. I just couldn't lie in bed any longer."

"Well, you're supposed to! You were rushing off to settle things with whoever hit you and ran, right?! Don't be crazy! Lean on us once in a while! Just tell me what they look like, and I'll tie 'em up in chains and drag 'em behind the van!"

"That's, uh...concerning. Besides, that's not the situation now. Where's Karisawa?"

"She's out looking for you right now! We'd better call her, or..."

"Tell her to come to this apartment right away. Either that or to go straight home and stay there. And...could you text the same thing to Azusa, too?" asked Kadota. His dad had his phone at the moment, so he had no means of contacting them himself.

Yumasaki started to get in touch with Karisawa, driven by the panicked look on Kadota's face.

"Damn, man, what's going on, then?" Togusa muttered.

The look on Kadota's face grew even darker. "The other reason I came here…is because there's something I need to talk to Celty about."

"The Headless Rider?"

"Yeah… The thing is, I'm pretty sure I know who's calling the shots for the guys who ran me over." Kadota grunted, gripping the bridge of his nose. "I saw a couple of 'em, just from taking a taxi…"

"…You saw what?" Togusa asked, but Kadota bypassed the question.

"The whole damn neighborhood…is in a real bad state right now."

♂♀

Russia Sushi, interior, late night

"Shizuo's one thing, but Vorona skipping her shift without permission, too? Sure was a lonely round today," griped Shizuo and Vorona's direct superior at work, Tom Tanaka, as he sipped hot green tea at a marble counter.

The restaurant was about to close, and the only customers left were Tom and a man with no hair sitting farther down the counter.

"Thanks to that attack, the cop cars are flyin' left and right down the streets. It's a dangerous world out there these days." He grunted. He didn't know yet that Shizuo had already been released from police custody. Normally, Tom would be the second person he'd contact after his brother, but with the confusion over Vorona, he apparently hadn't reached out yet.

So Tom, who still believed Shizuo was in jail, sat all alone at the counter of Russia Sushi, nursing a late dinner. When Denis, the head chef, learned that Vorona had skipped work without warning, he bowed to Tom. "Sorry about her. We'll give her a good scolding the next time she shows her face in here."

"No, it's fine. This is our company's issue anyway. Plus, I bet Vorona's shocked about what happened with Shizuo, too."

Simon returned from cleaning up the private booths now that the restaurant had cleared out. He shrugged his broad shoulders. "Oh, Shizuo, he good guy. He get vindication. What means vindication? Same as vacation? Or vegetation? You want vegetable roll? Today you can pay in Japanese yendication."

"Wait, are there days you *don't* accept yen? And I appreciate the offer, but I can't spend any more money..."

"You don't worry about it! I put it on tab! You need desperate measures in time of desperation!"

"I swear, you're a whole lot better at Japanese than you let on..."

At the end of this rather typical chat, Tom paid his bill and got up to leave. When he opened the door, he looked outside first.

"...Hmm?" He stopped in his tracks.

It wasn't that anything had crossed his field of view. But when he scanned the scenery of the city, he received an overwhelming impression of something being *off*.

Huh? The hell? Something's...weird.

He slowly examined the area but couldn't identify the source of the feeling. It seemed less like the scenery itself, though, and more like the people in it.

Huh? Then he picked up on it. *Is it just me, or is it...crowded? Huh? I mean, this place is closing up for the night, so...*

He pulled out his phone and checked the time. It was already after midnight. But there was an unsettling amount of foot traffic for this hour. Even during summer vacation, when young adults were sure to be out for the nightlife, why would it be so bustling, especially when the cops were racing around?

It almost felt like a nine o'clock crowd to Tom. Then he noticed that one distant man was watching him.

"Hmm?"

He didn't recognize the man. And yet, there was *something* about him. It was one man in a group of men and women standing at the corner of a parking garage behind the locksmith.

Tom readjusted his glasses and took a few steps for a closer look.

Oh...I know I've seen him before. Probably from one of our debt-collection headshots... But I don't think he had that hotshot host-club haircut before...

Suddenly, there was a different man within his view. A pedestrian dressed like a salaryman who had noticed Tom and was approaching with a smile.

"Huh?"

At first he thought the man was heading for the restaurant right behind him, but it was past last call, and they'd taken down the welcoming curtain over the doorway. And the salaryman wasn't looking at the building; he was looking *directly at Tom*.

What's up? Is this guy drunk? he wondered, staring closely at the man.

His face was indeed a red color. But it wasn't actually his skin that was red.

It was the whites of his eyes, bloodshot to an extreme shade of red.

"?!"

Something was wrong. Tom took a step back, wanting to return inside.

But the salaryman began to run now, sprinting at him. He wasn't carrying anything. But there was something dangerous and aggressive in his movements—and then his hand darted out to reveal nails sharpened to sawtooth points, either bitten or clipped into shape, that hunted for Tom's soft skin.

"Whoa!!" Tom yelped. But the man's body stopped short just before the nails would have made contact.

"...?"

Simon's large hand had closed around the man's arm.

"Oh, sir, you no fight here. Eat sushi is better, but we closed now. You come back tomorrow, have good time. We make market price special just for you," Simon said. He let go and pushed the man's chest.

The salaryman lost his balance and stumbled backward several steps. Then Simon grabbed Tom's arm instead and pulled him back into the building.

"Huh? Wait!"

The door closed, and Simon turned the lock.

"...What's going on?"

The last customer in the place, the man with the shaved head, looked at Shizuo and Tom curiously.

Simon spoke a few words of Russian to Denis. Rather uncharacteristically, there was no smile on Simon's face; Denis scowled, too, when he heard the message, and he looked through the windows to see what was happening outside.

Then, in his capacity as business manager, Denis warned the bald man and Tom, "Sirs, you're better off not going out."

"What does that mean?" asked the other man. The chef gestured with his eyes to the window. Tom and the man turned to look.

"..."

"Whoa, what the hell is that?" Tom exclaimed, while the bald man went silent.

The view outside the building was the same as it ever was.

Except for one thing...

Slow-moving crowds of people, all with bloodshot eyes, and *all staring right at them.*

$$♂♀$$

Automated parking garage, Ikebukuro

"Tch...screwed that one up," cursed Takashi Nasujima, who made a big show of being disappointed. "But he definitely reacted like he recognized my face. It was a good thing I checked before I run across Shizuo Heiwajima. Guess I should keep the disguise on."

Nasujima put a face mask and sunglasses on to hide his features. "Can't let it get out that I'm around town. I've got to slip Saika into that guy with the dreadlocks. He might come in handy as an ace up my sleeve against Shizuo," he chuckled.

Next to him, Shijima shivered violently. "What the hell is this...? They're all like *them*..."

He was thinking of how the members of Amphisbaena had looked when Izaya Orihara's subordinate had sliced them up. Earthworm and the rest of them had had glowing red eyes, as though their bodies had been taken over by aliens, and they'd followed the orders of the one who had cut them.

"You don't have to worry about it. I've instructed them not to cut you. For now."

"Er, uh, okay..."

Nasujima didn't explain anything about Saika to Shijima. Of course, a blanket reassurance only made him more anxious. Nasujima then put even more pressure on Shijima by asking, "By the way, have you fully infiltrated the Dollars by now? Did the *plan* go well?"

"Huh? Oh…yes. I think."

"I wasn't asking you to *think*."

"S-sorry, sir!" Shijima said on instinct, eliciting a laugh from Nasujima.

"Look, don't get so formal with me. For one thing, Saika is extremely inflexible; when you're being controlled, the red eyes are obvious and unavoidable. It's valuable having people like you, Shijima, who can help us out while in a normal state."

"O-okay…"

"I honestly didn't expect to grow so many 'grandchildren' at this rate, however. It was worth doing those experiments to find out that nails and teeth could be treated like Saika, too. All you really need is a bit of pain and fear. We won't need to take Kujiragi's route—we can even feast on the Awakusu-kai's turf."

"Ummm…if you've got all this power, why bother with the Awakusu-kai, when you can just take over the world…?"

Nasujima shook his head from side to side. "No, no, no, Shijima. It's not good to set your sights too high. Yes, it would be lovely to control the entire world. But you see, I'm not looking to be a king. I just want a lot of money that can buy me a lot of comfort, and the ability to have my way with a well-endowed woman whenever I want. That's all."

Shijima felt a bit gloomy; the absence of the phrase *woman I love* in that statement felt like a revelation of Nasujima's true nature. But it was true that the man had great power at his command.

If the street slashings started again, they would cause a big commotion, but he never hesitated. In a place without security cameras, he surrounded his targets with "grandchildren," and as soon as they panicked, he had them pierced with Saika blades—from small knives to claws and teeth, even little safety pins hidden in the palm. Anything would do.

It was as simple as that.

The reason the last time had become so public was that the targets had been cut so badly, they'd needed to go to the hospital to recuperate. Nasujima had realized that and done his best to experiment with methods to quickly but surreptitiously grow more grandchildren, until he had constructed this simple method.

In this one area, at least, Nasujima lived up to his credentials as a former teacher. He told the woman who was once his pupil, "I got this power all because of you. I'm grateful, Haruna."

He was speaking to Haruna Niekawa, who stood across from Shijima. He had once been a shining star to Haruna, and until yesterday, she might have passed out with excitement if she had heard him say those words.

But now she just smiled dully and didn't even turn to look at Nasujima. "...Right."

Shijima eyed her out of the corner of his vision and wondered, *This chick...used to work with Izaya Orihara, right? Awww, man, this is all crazy. I don't even know what's goin' on anymore.* He plunged into terrified, ignorant chaos, his face pale and sunken.

Meanwhile, Nasujima's barely exposed skin was bright and shiny. "It's gonna happen tomorrow. No, I guess it's technically today now... We're going to settle everything today, Haruna."

"...Right."

"I can't wait for that all to be done. Then I'll be able to give you *allll* the attention again, Haruna...," he said with a leer, licking his lips. His eyes traveled from Niekawa's face to her chest, and then lower.

Despite the gaze of pure lust sliding all over her skin, Haruna Niekawa merely stared into nothingness with bloodshot eyes and spoke in a voice with no affect.

"...Yes, *Mother.*"

It was the word that proved her free will had been eaten away by Saika.

If it was love that helped spread Saika, then Nasujima was indeed a man overflowing with it.

His love was very close to Saika's accursed love, a dedication to satisfying his own desires. It was a kind of twisted self-love that wasn't quite narcissism, but you could certainly call it a type of love.

At this point in time, Nasujima had about 2,300 of Saika's grandchildren under his control. There was no ideal, no vision behind this. The only thing they spread through the town was his own vulgar desire.

Without the restraint Kujiragi had, Nasujima's rampage showed no signs of slowing down. It corroded the neighborhood of Ikebukuro in the most twisted possible form.

♂♀

Ruined building

Something was happening in Ikebukuro.

Mikado felt that premonition so strongly that it might as well have been conviction.

While the Blue Squares were napping in their cars or nearby twenty-four-hour manga cafés, Mikado remained inside the abandoned building. The ones who stayed up at night were down on the first floor, but Mikado still wasn't in the mood to sleep.

There was the evening news story about the abandoned severed head. Then the report about a police vehicle being attacked in Ikebukuro. Lastly, the recent chat room incident.

On the backside of these events involving himself and the Dollars, *something* else was moving forward in Ikebukuro. And it was undoubtedly something with an occult, magical bent, like Celty.

Mikado was mildly surprised that he didn't find himself elated by this situation. His old middle school self—or even his self at the first Dollars meetup—would have been thrilled at the idea of a new life just around the corner, and his heart would have been jumping out of his chest with joy.

So why was now different? If he placed his hand over his heart, he felt no quickening there, no stirring of the blood. If anything, his current mental state was closer to *Who cares?*

He was worried about Celty, his acquaintance. But it was a very commonplace and commonsense feeling, that mundane concern about someone he knew being a victim.

Mikado was at least a little alarmed and confused about the disappearance of the version of himself that longed for the abnormal.

It's so strange. It feels like I'm turning into something other than myself.

On the day of the skirmish between the Dollars and Toramaru, from the very moment he'd driven that ballpoint pen through Aoba's hand, he'd felt a kind of light dizziness at all times. It grew stronger by the day, until at last he was standing before scenery he'd never seen before.

Normally, he might panic. He might deny what was happening. Insist that this couldn't be possible. That he hadn't meant for it to be this way.

But Mikado Ryuugamine accepted it all.

He might end up killing a person.

He might get killed instead.

He might kill himself.

He accepted even this present situation, so steeped in predictions and premonitions, as a part of his ordinary daily life.

But I don't want to die, and I definitely don't want to be a murderer, he thought, a sign that even as he accepted the situation, his mind was still functioning properly. *But since I've got this now, it would be a waste if I didn't go ahead and use it.*

It was through this imitation of typical everyday thought processes that Mikado found himself in possession of something that was absolutely abnormal and atypical for Japan.

Depending on where you lived, it *could* be a totally ordinary tool. And in fact, the man named Horada had possessed one when the Yellow Scarves and the Dollars were at war. But Mikado had just missed the chance to see it in action.

He sighed and gingerly picked up the object, which was wrapped in newspaper.

"I bet...that when you're not going to fire it, it's a bad idea to put your finger on the trigger."

He was holding a gleaming black automatic pistol.

What Izumii had brought to him as a "present" was none other than a weapon that was a crime to even possess in Japan.

In a sense, it was small beans at this point. When Horada had shot Shizuo, he certainly hadn't killed him. And Celty had defended herself against far more powerful rifle shots. Even tonight, Shizuo had stared down the barrel of Vorona's gun.

But these incidents had all happened to Shizuo and Celty. And when the boy named Mikado Ryuugamine grabbed this gun, it indicated a major shift in the standing of the Dollars as a whole.

Obviously, with guns being illegal, it was not the sort of thing your average person could pick up and use. Trying to actually aim with it and hit a moving target? Nearly impossible.

But that was the sort of thing that could be improved upon, depending on the circumstances. If you knew how to hold it steady and pull the trigger, you could do the job even if you were an amateur, given a close enough proximity. At a slight distance, Horada had succeeded in hitting Shizuo Heiwajima's side and leg.

If you had a sleeping target, you could kill them for sure. But only if you had the guts to go through with it.

And if you were going to stand next to someone and shoot them, it wouldn't be that different from using a knife. Yet, there was no tool better for threatening than this.

Most likely, Aozaki had chosen to pass the weapon along through Izumii to see what Mikado Ryuugamine would do with this tool. Even by the Awakusu-kai's standards, this was highly unorthodox.

And Mikado, having been given this gun for unorthodox reasons, now gazed upon it with very orthodox eyes. It was the same way one gazed at a newfangled remote from when TVs went digital and the number of buttons multiplied. There was no special excitement or fear in his eyes, just ordinary examination.

"Guns are scary. I can't stop trembling," he said, the kind of thing a normal boy might say. But on the inside, a different feeling was blooming.

What is this? I'm supposed to be afraid of it...but right now, I feel much more afraid of Mr. Akabayashi from yesterday, he thought, which was rather out of place. Then he murmured to himself, still very matter-of-fact:

"I better look up the right way to shoot this thing online."

He didn't need any guts for that.

He'd gotten all of that out of the way the moment he'd opened the door to the abnormal on the day of the Dollars' first meeting.

Mikado Ryuugamine could fire that gun.

But who to point it at? Or what to use it for? That, he was still uncertain of.

Among the options he had for targets of this gun, he could see the vague image of his own face—but at this stage, Mikado could not choose anyone.

He didn't even know whether that was a good thing or a sign of his own weakness.

But knowing that having the gun was a form of proud, doomed resistance—Mikado Ryuugamine decided to make an enemy of his own weakness and everything caught in its vortex.

And perhaps Ikebukuro itself.

♂♀

Morning arrived in Tokyo.

But whether the clock hand hit the sixth hour or the seventh, sunlight did not fall upon the neighborhood of Ikebukuro.

Pure black shadow enveloped the space over the top of the city, a cover that put the word *cloudy* to shame.

It was like the night still continued, and the alien, bewildering experience frightened residents and made major headlines.

Morning never arrived for Ikebukuro on this day.

It was explained for the mass audience as a "natural phenomenon caused by the effects of a special type of sandstorm" and would eventually be forgotten as another freak event. But it was, in fact, completely supernatural in nature.

In a town where the sky was covered by a fairy's shadow, a story of twisted love quietly came to a close.

Durarara!! x12—End

Author: Ryohgo Narita

©2013 Ryohgo Narita

AFTERWORD

I'm sorry—it didn't end at the twelfth volume...!

So anyway, hello, I'm Ryohgo Narita.

In the previous volume, I wrote about how I wanted to mark the end of a story in Volume 12, but thanks to a flare-up of my many bad habits, I ended up with too much content to fit into one book, so I had to split it again.

Volume 13 will be rather thick, and it should complete the story of Mikado, Anri, and Masaomi for now, so I hope you look forward to it...

Now, let's talk about this story, content spoilers included.

We ended off with Izaya and Shizuo in quite a state, but if you think about it, it feels rather potent, as those two might not have faced off directly (in the novels) since the situation at Izaya's apartment in Volume 2.

Even I'm not sure who will win or what the outcome will mean in terms of life or death, so just wait for Volume 13!

Also, I do remember having a crosstalk interview with Kazuma Kamachi of *A Certain Magical Index* before and saying something like "What would be the point of giving Celty her head back and turning this into some wild supernatural occult manga? Ha-ha-ha-ha-ha!" To Mr. Kamachi and everyone who read that interview, I am so sorry! We are at the wild supernatural occult stage!

Even I didn't think Celty would get her head back, but once I realized I was putting Shingen into the city with freedom of movement, and that of course he would do something like that, it essentially became inevitable.

As for what will happen to Celty in Volume 13, and whether she'll lose all her memories of Shinra, and whether morning will ever come to Ikebukuro—not to mention all the other squabbles happening outside of Mikado's vicinity, and how they'll wind up, and who will laugh and who will cry at the end—the answers are all blowing in the wind at this moment.

I will be making my way toward Volume 13, one step at a time, and hoping that at the very end it is hope that will come blowing back our way.